ETERNAL FIRE

ANGEL FIRE, BOOK 6

MARIE JOHNSTON

LE PUBLISHING

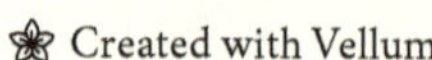 Created with Vellum

Persephone's zest for life and love of bad jokes were quelled by parents who made her feel worthless. So she proved them right and became the angelic version of a rich mean girl. Until she trusted the wrong person and suffered wounds that'll scar her for the rest of her eternal life.

Urban used to be an angelic warrior who was equal parts work and play. One day he'd had enough of a certain spoiled angel and said something he couldn't take back. And then he found himself standing over the beautiful female, who had injuries no immortal should suffer.

During recovery, the warrior who'd verbally gutted Persephone stayed by her bedside. He even coaxed her to tell jokes again. He built her up instead of tearing her down. He helped her wonder *what if*.

What if her parents and the rest of the realm were wrong? What if a privileged angel with no talent could make something of herself? What if she deserved love? Urban's with her the whole way—until danger threatens the realm and he's the one blocking her path.

CHAPTER 1

Persephone Nassim glared at the glass of water on the table. She was thirsty, but she'd have to cross the room to get a drink, and it was really unfair.

"Unfair" had been the theme of her life lately. Or maybe all the crap that'd happened to her was perfectly justified. She'd been a useless angel, and she was paying the price of privilege and a selfish personality.

With a sigh, she scooted to the edge of the seat. She groaned as she rose, the weight of her wings hanging on the scars on her back. Tears pricked the backs of her eyelids, and she wanted to sob. She'd wasted a lot of time crying—for herself, mostly. No one else had been hurt by her stupidity. Thanks to the warriors who had saved her. The angelic Numen realm protectors, who also hunted demons on the earthly realm, had prevented the trouble she would have caused by being unaware she was being used.

Biting her lips, she took a step. It hurt to hold her wings still, and it was agony when they moved. A real damned-if-she-did, damned-if-she-didn't scenario for an angel to be in.

Why'd this marble mansion have to be so big, so empty and useless? The place was like she'd once been. Ornamental. Decorative. Purposeless.

No. The house had a purpose as the place for her to recover from the angel-fire burns she'd sustained when a senator she should've been able to trust tried to sell her to angelic traffickers. Before her injuries, she'd roamed the realm with other spoiled adult children of senators. Most angels had roles that served the realm, but she didn't. Not then. Not now. And her parents hadn't exactly encouraged her to find one.

This house should've been a home. Instead, Persephone had felt as worthless here as everywhere else in the realm. So when Senator Juliette Colbert had taken an interest in her, Persephone hadn't seen that the senator's interest wasn't in her as a person. She had assumed the senator was genuine in both her leadership of the realm and in the Numen residents' role as angelic spirits who watched over the human realm.

To be fair, Persephone had never considered living up to the expectations of her birth. Everyone else could cover for her since she was useless anyway, she'd thought. Her lack of ambition had made her an easy target for a traitorous, selfish bitch like Juliette Colbert.

Persephone had gone from being a spoiled, privileged young female to being sold to the highest demon bidder—by her own kind. Now she was paying for the way she'd lived down to others' beliefs about her.

Maybe she should've known Numen were working with the underworld realm of Daemon to feed their own self-interests and dark desires and to pad the accounts they'd been growing for decades or centuries. She should've realized being daft wasn't the most dangerous character trait in the realm. Numen weren't divine angels, so of course they could be corrupted.

She'd been too oblivious to know. Something that shouldn't have been bad—not assuming the worst of others—but that she'd suffered for.

She gritted her teeth as she took slow steps across the room, fire lacing her back. The expensive salve she'd survived on was no longer a help. She was full of scar tissue and angry nerves. There were no more open sores or gaping wounds, but she was weak and tender in a way she had never been before—and she'd been weak before the attack.

Her mother swept into the room, her startled gaze landing on her. "Oh, Persephone. You should've rung."

The bell. Persephone would rather toss the little silver bell out the window. The dainty device her parents had given her to summon them when she needed something was the sound of her helplessness.

Mother, please help me to the bathroom.

Father, can you pick up my book? It fell.

I'm done with my plate, but I can't carry it even across the house. Please, help.

She would've ruthlessly wielded the bell before she'd been betrayed. Before she'd been seen as nothing more than a leaky bucket of confidential information. A cow to trade. She'd have run ragged the mansion's staff. But her parents had let their employees go rather than have witnesses to Persephone in pain and toddling around the place.

Heaven forbid anyone realize the members of the mighty Nassim family were not divine angels in a realm of nondivine angels.

"I've got it." Mother beat her to the glass.

Persephone suppressed a groan. The more she moved, the better she'd recover, but her parents coddled her. She'd find it less insufferable if their care stemmed from concern, not a lack of confidence.

She accepted the glass and drained its contents. Mother plucked it from her hands, worry puckering the corners of her eyes.

"I'll refill it and put it by the chair. I'll be right back to help you sit." Mother rushed out toward the kitchen.

Persephone was tempted to close her eyes, wishing she could will water from the floor. Numen's natural energy powered the electronics, but the plumbing was based on the human realm, coming from miraculously filled wells in the outermost ring. Far away from the fountain of plasmatic angel fire in the middle of Numen. A place that made her back ache with the thought of it.

Would she ever be able to think about angel fire without pain?

Their kind's natural healing ability allowed them to live for centuries, but it was useless against angel-fire wounds, and angel fire was one of the few things that could harm a Numen beyond self-healing.

"I can refill it." She shuffled after her mother.

"No." The older woman turned and shooed Persephone away. "You need rest. I'll be right back." The last part was spoken slowly, like Persephone would have a hard time understanding the concept.

"That's all I've been doing."

Mother turned, wearing that *I'm so much smarter than you* look that had grated on Persephone's nerves more since she'd been injured. "Honey, you could've been killed. I hope you remember that."

There were many times Persephone had wished the angel fire had burned it all away—her life, her shame, the pain. Angel fire burned until it ceased to exist. Nothing could extinguish it; no Numen crystal could contain it. And Persephone had waited out the agonizing seconds, wondering just what she'd done to earn the blistering pain.

The worst part now was knowing. She'd been a miserable, hateful female. So much had become clear that day.

"I need to do things for myself. I need to move, or I won't be able to function like Felicia Hancock."

Felicia had endured severe injuries that had left her scarred, and her broken wings hadn't been properly repaired. For years afterward, she stayed away from the realm. Now she was back, a senator like Persephone's mother and happily mated. Instead of flying, Felicia either walked or caught rides with her handsome warrior mate. She gave zero fucks about what others thought of her misshapen wings. She was brave. She had a purpose. She hadn't wasted most of her life.

"You're not Felicia."

A different kind of hurt whipped through Persephone. She heard what her mother didn't say. It was in her tone. *You're not smart like Felicia. You're not strong like Felicia. You're not resourceful like Felicia. You're not resilient like Felicia.*

Felicia's father had been a senator, and after her mother died, Persephone's mother had doted on Felicia and her sister. Those females rated higher in Mother's opinion than her own daughter ever had.

Giving up, Persephone turned to resume her seat on the couch, but she couldn't hold back a wince. The twist in her torso pulled on the tough scar tissue. Would it ever become less painful?

"Oh, honey, why don't you go to your room and lie down? It's getting late."

Because she'd been restricted to her room for months. The sitting area was an upgrade. Downright adventurous. "The couch is fine," she gritted out.

"But you need to change positions," Mother said.

"I'm standing, aren't I?"

There was the sigh. The long-suffering exhale her mother reserved for the times she felt Persephone was especially unreachable. The sigh destroyed any sense of improvement Persephone had made within herself. Her own parents thought she was worthless. She'd tried to free herself from their opinion, but this was where she'd ended up—more dependent on them than ever.

"Fine," she mumbled. "I'll go to bed."

Her mother was right, and she didn't look forward to sitting on the backless couch and getting up again. A necessary task, but her back ached. Plus, nightfall brought *him*.

Urban Moulin. The warrior she'd low-key crushed on for years and who'd saved her. He'd come to check on her and hadn't been daunted when her parents turned him away. Instead, he'd appeared at her second-story window, a terrifying visitor until his stocky shape registered in her brain. She'd committed his muscles to memory along with the leather-and-soap scent that lingered long after he'd removed his training gear and holsters.

How did he dress when he was on Earth and blending in with humans?

One of the reasons she'd agreed to accompany Senator Colbert to Earth was so she could get used to the human way of life and become more independent. Perhaps she would've found a role that suited her on Earth.

Instead, she'd been tricked, and Urban had helped to save her. Then he'd rescued her again by sitting with her and just talking during those long, pain-filled, sleepless nights. For the first time since she'd been a kid, she remembered her earliest identity.

Persephone Nassim had been a girl who liked a good dad joke and loved learning. Who hadn't been told that her jokes weren't funny and that senator families were held to higher standards. Who hadn't been taught politics, compared to the daughters of other senators, and found lacking.

"I'll pull your sheets back." Mother rushed ahead of her.

What would it have been like if Mother or Father had been this caring when she was younger? If they hadn't spent days and evenings with other senators and their families, leaving her with employees who had treated her like an ornament they didn't know how to handle?

"Thank you," she said dutifully, hoping Mother wouldn't flit around her room and keep Urban away.

His secret visits were life, as Persephone craved real conversation during the months of otherwise being treated like a damaged glass doll with a head full of air.

She changed from her backless robe to a backless sleeping shift. Lately, she'd taken more care with what she wore. Her mother had cut the backs out of several of her tops, gowns, and robes so she could step into them and pull them up. Getting her wings and arms through the holes was difficult, but it was better than nearly blacking out from the agony of putting her arms over her head. Persephone had spent her days sewing the hems. Hiring out for the task would've meant admitting something was wrong, like a neon sign above the mansion announcing to the realm that the Nassims' clueless daughter had almost died.

She carefully crawled into bed and lay on her side so her wings were supported by the mattress. Her mother pulled the satin sheet over her body and smoothed it down.

"There. Time to rest. You've had a trying day." Mother bent and kissed her forehead.

Her day had been no such thing. Persephone let her eyelids flutter shut. "Good night, Mother."

When she was alone, her eyes shot open. She watched the balcony. He never came at the same time, but he'd likely arrive soon. She ran her hand over her hair. It was hard to look appealing when half her face was plastered against the pillow. She couldn't sleep on her back yet, and she didn't want to be on her stomach during her time with him. Hard to visit that way—and her scars would show.

One night, Urban would show and she'd be sitting up and have her typical joke ready. Perhaps she could even be standing. Walking around. Her back would be bare and her scars visible, though. He'd seen the angel fire burning her, so what was left had to be better than that, but she didn't want his thoughts to be on her attack. She wanted more from him than support. Friendship for one. She was afraid to think of how far beyond friendship she'd be willing to go.

Letting some of her giddy nerves out on a long breath, she settled into the bedding. Soon. He'd be here soon, and he'd help her feel better like he always did.

URBAN WAS IN THE BARRACKS, putting away the weapons he'd been cleaning. He kept a bunk just for this. His house wasn't his favorite place to be, but he didn't want to drag demon blood home. Had his knives been dirty? No, but ever since his team had rooted out a corrupt senator and cleared the name of a former enforcer, the realm had been quiet. There were warrior teams roaming Earth and keeping it as free of demon influence as possible, but since his former team leader had become director of all warriors, his team had become more like a special forces unit. Reserved for particular missions.

The lull his team was in would have driven him nuts, but he'd been keeping busy in a way no one knew about.

He was packing away the last of his weapons, tucking the final dagger into its holster to slide under his bunk and marveling for the thousandth time how different things were. His whole team had slept in the bunks around this one. Now those beds were filled with single warriors like him, ones who couldn't be bothered to care for a house in Numen when there were demons to hunt on Earth.

Urban's motivation had been the same. Staying in the barracks was easier. Simpler for a warrior residing in two different realms. Now that his age was approaching a century, his life just seemed…empty. Most of the time he could ignore the feeling, but then a rookie would move in, all optimistic and bloodthirsty, and he'd mentally roll his eyes and try to ignore them. Young angels made his ass feel like he was half a millennium old.

All his warrior teammates except for Ransom, the newest member, were mated. But Ransom had raised one of their former team members, Sierra, and he'd become more like a dad to those around him. Besides, Ransom still lived in his house in one of the outer rings of the realm, the same place where Sierra had grown up.

Ransom poked his head through the doorway across from Urban's bunk. "Hey, man. Glad to catch you before some female got her nails into you."

Urban smirked like it was what he'd been doing every night for the last several months. The others assumed he was out getting laid, and yeah, that used to be the case. But his nightly disappearance was a lot more innocent these days. The female occupying his attention had surprised him with her depth and love of punny jokes. "I'll be heading out soon."

Ransom gave him a regretful shake of his head. "Sorry, but Director Vale wants to see us."

Urban's gut clenched. Typically, he was mission ready every second of the day, but did they have to meet now?

He could visit Persephone later. She might be asleep, but she'd told him to wake her if he ran late.

Masking his annoyance, he shoved his dagger into the top of his boot. Most Numen wore white robes, but warriors preferred to dress like they were ready to hit the training ring in tactical pants and long-sleeved shirts with boots.

"Sure." He fell in step with Ransom, their wings high behind them, as they walked down the long marble hall. They exited the building and headed for the headquarters and the director's office.

Acid churned in Urban's stomach. At this time of day, the director was usually at home, buried in his mate. But he was in his office instead, so just how bad was the news?

Ransom tapped on the director's door.

"Enter." The gravelly voice was Director Vale's new norm.

They walked in. Nothing about the reason for the meeting could be deduced from the director's expression. Before his injuries, he'd been a scowling bastard. After he'd been hit with angel fire on the side of his face, he gave off nothing but pissed-off vibes. The guy was happily mated, but he looked at a warrior like they'd kicked his dog.

Urban had been on the team with the director at the time of his injury. He'd witnessed what his boss had gone through, but it'd taken on new meaning while seeing Persephone dealing with what had happened to her.

Bryant Vale had been a seasoned warrior when he'd been ambushed and his vial of angel fire turned on him. Persephone was a young female who'd been sheltered from the worst Numen life had to offer, much less the hell demons could create.

"Right." The director pushed back from his desk. His wings were folded behind him, highlighting the granite set to his face. "I have a job for you two."

"Can we do it in the morning?" Urban practically hadn't missed a night with Persephone since her injury. Definitely not in the last few months.

Their relationship consisted of him showing up on her deck and talking quietly so her parents didn't catch them like they were lovesick teens instead of… He didn't know what he and Persephone were. But she deserved more than suddenly being ditched for a night or longer. It wasn't like he had her number or could ask around to get it. Did she even have a phone? A lot of Numen liked to use energy-driven phones, no cell towers needed. But Persephone wasn't known to leave the realm much before the incident.

Director Vale shot him a disgruntled glare that said if it could wait, they wouldn't be in his bloody office when he could be at home with his mate. "No. I need you to go back to Las Vegas."

Urban wanted to groan. Since the fallen angel who'd developed his own cult working with demons from the underworld had set up shop in a nightclub in Vegas, Urban had spent too much time there. Maybe it was the sense that this mission wasn't a one-and-done demon-possession hunt, but he didn't want another mission that'd take him away from Numen for days and weeks, maybe even months.

"Whatever you need," Ransom said, ever the male willing to do what needed to be done. The go-to team member. The warrior who should've been leading his own team years ago but had played Mr. Mom to Sierra instead. "We're ready."

Ransom needed to shut up.

The director's gaze hadn't left Urban. He sensed something was up, but Urban forced himself to nod. It wasn't the director's business.

"All right, then," Director Vale eventually continued. "There's an angel snooping where she shouldn't. She's been looking into that bastard Jameson and the even more evil Andy."

The fallen angel and his accountant, a criminal mastermind. No random Numen resident should've known about them. The senate had made sure the threat the realm faced hadn't gotten out.

"They're both dead," Urban said bluntly.

"Yes. And so, we hoped, was the story behind them. But this female thinks she can uncover some dirt." Director Vale flicked a finger up. "I want to know why." Another finger. "I want to know what she plans to do with the information. Sierra's got a bead on her. If you leave now, you might be able to find her."

Ransom sat straighter at the mention of his daughter. Sierra and her human mate, Boone, might be in the middle of nowhere Montana, but Sierra could hack her way into camera systems all over the world.

"The female has been seen in the area where Fall From Grace stood."

The nightclub Jameson's cult had been centered around. Again, no regular Numen schmuck should've known about it. "The place burned down. The site was cleaned and sold a year ago."

"Exactly. And she's not talking to regular folks. Sierra's linked the female's contacts to former members of Jameson's little following."

Ransom cocked his head. "The ones who visited the club to dance and flirt with danger or those who allowed themselves to host demons?"

"Yes." Director Vale flipped his phone around. A grainy screenshot of a young female with long, dark hair, wide brown eyes, and more tits than she knew what to do with.

Urban gave zero fucks about the female other than the pain in his ass she was causing. "With that rack, we should be able to pick her out easy enough."

Ransom gave a disapproving grunt. Urban lifted a challenging brow. He hadn't meant to be disrespectful, but stating the obvious and using frank words didn't sap his brainpower. He had somewhere else to be and no way to tell Persephone he couldn't get there.

"Do we have a name?" Ransom asked in his steady *this is how it's done* way.

"Elodie Rogers. Her parents sell produce in the market, and she's been through chaperone training."

A girl who guided human souls to the light at the end of the tunnel was creeping around Vegas?

"Elodie," Ransom said and peered closer at the photo. "I know her dad. He brings the best melons back from Earth to sell at the market. He was telling me the other day he wished she'd work with them instead of working on Earth."

Urban barely knew the Rogers' first names, much less that they had an adult kid.

"Well, she's not looking for fruit." The director tucked his phone back into his robe pocket. Ever since he'd taken the director position, he wore the standard garb of the realm more often. Claimed it made the senate take him more seriously and that it was all the politicking he planned to do. "She's going to cause trouble. It's amazing we've been able to keep all the shite that's happened between us and the senate quiet, but if Elodie keeps sticking her nose where she shouldn't, a demon's going to claw it off."

And the rest of the realm might learn how badly some of their senators had been corrupted. How close the realm was to demonic influence. And worse, that angel-demon offspring were running around, able to enter the realm, a privilege forbidden to full demons from Daemon.

One of the demon-angels—Sierra—had been raised in Numen by the male standing next to Urban.

Then to learn the other halfling, Sandeen, controlled the ore mines in Daemon and was the realm's contact for the steel used to forge its weapons?

They'd shit.

Especially if they learned that the senate used to trade with Sandeen's very evil, very diabolic father. Willingly.

"Sierra just notified me that the female's around the location of the old club tonight," the director said. "She's going to hurt herself if she keeps drifting through Las Vegas at night. But you two need to find what she's up to." The director's whiskey-hued gaze landed on Urban. "Now."

Damn. He needed to forget the urge to see Persephone and get his head in the mission. He couldn't go into a big city at night, distracted, when demons might be out to play.

"Got it."

The director's steady look didn't leave him. "I'm not interrupting anything, am I?"

"No," Urban said. The director cocked the brow on the

unscarred side of his face. He could sense the lie, but would he keep prodding?

"Go," he ordered before Urban and Ransom walked out into the night.

It would be around the same time on Earth. Much of Numen's work was done in the US—demons loved capitalism—and the days and nights coincided.

Urban heaved a sigh. He had all his weapons. A few daggers strapped on his body and a crystal vial of angel fire around his neck. He was ready to go.

Ransom spun on him, his wings already morphed into his back. Invisible and out of the way. Ransom was dressed the same as Urban—tactical gear in dark colors. But when he propped his hands on his hips, Urban felt like he was going to get detention. "Is your head in the game?"

"Am I going to get extra chores if it isn't?"

Ransom's blond brows drew together. With his curly blond hair, he looked like a chiseled cupid. "If I have to. I've got a few dad jokes to go with it."

Hearing he had jokes was like an arrow to Urban's chest. He wasn't falling in love, but he cared for Persephone. He'd grown just as fond of her jokes as he was of watching her laugh when she told them. No one would believe him, but she had a bright personality and a sweet sense of humor under her sinful curves and arrogant expression.

He'd had a good joke prepared for tonight. "No jokes," he said gruffly. "I had plans, and this Elodie stepped all over them."

"It's the life of a warrior."

"It's not. It's the life of Director Vale's personal team." Warriors had a schedule. They were on Earth and then they were off. They weren't perpetually on call like Urban and the rest had been for years.

"Have you talked to him about it?"

Ransom and his fucking discussions. He was so even-keeled. Before Urban's best bud and fellow teammate Bronx had fallen in love, the two warriors would fuck around in the human realm during their time off. When they were called to a mission, they'd be ready to go. All they were walking away from were random hookups.

But now that he and Ransom were the only single team members, they were the easy ones to send out. Bronx was tucked away with his mate. Team Leader Dionna was still on Earth with hers. Harlowe and Sandeen were also on Earth—safer for Sandeen and probably for Numen. Sierra was a fallen and couldn't reside in Numen, so she lived in Montana with her human mate, Boone. Jagger and Felicia were probably already in bed. And the director didn't go into the field anymore.

"No. Why would I talk to him?"

Ransom's gaze was steady. "He should know of possible issues."

"No issues other than you're taking forever. We've got a melon peddler's daughter to catch."

Annoyance crossed Ransom's face. He was startlingly easy to read. Urban hadn't witnessed him killing demons yet. Ransom had a solid reputation, but all Urban had seen from him were kind smiles and expressions that broadcasted his emotions. Not the strongest qualities for a warrior.

Ransom gestured to his black cargo pants. "We should change to blend with Vegas nightlife better."

"Only if you expect to be seen."

He rolled his eyes. "Fine. I'll have to hang on to you when we transcend. I've never been to Fall From Grace."

Regret gnawed at Urban's insides. Ransom was catching the brunt of his irritation. If Urban told him exactly what was going on, he'd probably help Urban swing by and tell Persephone he had to leave. But Urban couldn't let his secret out. His time with the injured angel was all his, and if people thought he was catching feelings, they'd have expectations: Were they dating? Was he in love? Would they mate?

He held back a shudder. No mating. Not for him. Syncing his life force with someone without a guarantee sounded like a horrible idea. The special mark sync mates got on their wrists was barely a promise. More like an idea. "Hey, you two might work together for eternity." But if the couple bonded—mated—they could struggle with love as badly as humans.

He'd seen how a sync bond between a couple soured, and he wouldn't choose that for himself. If some female developed the sync brand on her wrist for him, he'd deal with it when the time came. He'd propose they bonded in name only and that she leave him the fuck alone.

But he didn't have to worry about mating, just leaving a lonely angel without a word. Hopefully, Persephone didn't wait up for him.

CHAPTER 2

Silently crying for half the night had accomplished nothing. She'd waited for Urban for hours, staying awake, terrified she'd miss him. Needing to see him after being smothered by her mother.

But he didn't show.

She'd had plenty of time to think during the time she was in bed. About her parents. About how Urban was the *only* person who'd visited her since the injury. And finally, about what the hell she was going to do about it.

She had two options. The simplest was to go to sleep, wake in the morning, and limp to the main room to sit all day while her mother and father took turns waiting on her. And if she made a move to the front door, she'd be rushed back to a chair. Little Persephone was always better to be seen and not heard.

Or.

She could…do something else. Something like…

The last two hours until dawn were composed of plans. Persephone hated being doted on. She hated being locked away. She hated being thought of as weak or simple or selfish or anything else that didn't feel like her but that she was compelled to live up to. Or down to?

Either way, she was done. Over it.

The rays of morning lit the room's shades. Stifling her groan, she rolled to the edge of the bed. Agony ripped through her back as she shifted her weight over her wings until she was sitting up, the bed supporting the injured appendages. Standing was the worst part of the day.

No longer. The worst part was being stood up by a quiet warrior who'd rebuffed her constantly before she'd been attacked.

And the final time, he'd rejected her in the market. His words still stung in her memories. *Why would I bother with a spoiled female who has absolutely no use in this realm or any other? Go find someone who won't look past your beauty to the emptiness underneath.*

The accuracy was worse than anything.

Biting her lip, she stood. Her throat thickened and she wanted to cry out, but then her parents would wake and stop her. She limped to the window, her scarred flesh adjusting to the weight of her wings. Fresh morning air surrounded her as she stepped outside onto the balcony.

Pale rays of light crossed the horizon. If she didn't want to be a spectacle, she'd have to get going. She crept to the edge. A million times, she had swan-dived off the platform and taken to the skies, but she hadn't flown for months.

Inch by inch, she spread her wings.

Almighty, it *hurt*. When her wings were unfurled, she leaped before she could talk herself out of it. As soon as her wing joints took her body's weight, she plummeted. The air whooshed out of her when she slammed into the ground. She couldn't cry out and bring attention to yet another failure. When she noisily sucked air in, she stuffed her face into the thick grass. A sob left her, and she was afraid to move her wings.

How much pain could one person take?

Gritting her teeth, she lifted her head. She knew exactly how much she could handle. Feeling parts of her skin and muscles burn up while she was fully conscious and scared out of her mind had given her an idea. A weak person wouldn't have survived what she had.

The realization emboldened her.

Pushing herself up, she made it to her knees. Instead of ignoring the agony, she leaned into it, used it to fuel her determination.

She was flying tonight, dammit.

Her eyes watered, or maybe she was crying, but she rose, the full weight of her wings hanging from her back.

"I am not weak," she ground through clenched teeth and took a step. Then another. Breathing in and out at regular intervals, she screwed her eyes shut and launched into the air.

A cry ripped from her lips, but she kept airborne, dipping until she worried she'd fly into the treetops. Soaring, she swooped and wove, air fluttering her feathers. She swore she could feel each feather twitch in the nerves of her back, but she kept going.

The few angels who were out were startled by the sight of her. The ones walking on the ground didn't notice her, and she was grateful for that one small grace. She should've changed out of her night shift, but she'd worn clothing more revealing to buy bananas. It'd have to do.

Rectangular marble buildings came into view, and she landed at the largest. The one that'd house the main office.

A moan wrenched from her lips when her feet touched down. Sweat dotted her brow, so she drew a shaky arm over her forehead. The night of missed sleep clutched at her body. Fire raced up and down her spine, but the dull ache that settled in wasn't worse than that on any other day of recovery.

A win was a win.

"Miss Nassim," a male's gritty voice said behind her.

She spun and went ramrod straight. A wince was immediate. "Shit, that hurts." She rolled her lips in, accustomed to hiding how much pain she felt.

The director of Numen's warriors had spoken, and he did nothing but lift his good brow at her reaction. And then he surprised her further. "It does. Pulls like a bitch for months."

Her knees turned rubbery, and she whispered, "You know."

Of course he did. His face showed proof he was one of the few beings in the realm to understand. The sheer relief of being seen was staggering. His response reinforced her decision to go there today.

"The recovery process from angel-fire burns still haunts my dreams." His stern expression softened. "It does get better, but the memories take forever to fade."

"Especially when Odessa's there to tuck you in at night." She didn't mean to sound bitter, but she had no one, and one of the angels she'd detested much of her life was with the stoic warrior director. Not only was Odessa smart, alluring, and a pure soul, she had the love of the handsome male with a face full of scars.

The director was good-looking in a way that made a female want to walk on the wild side. He wore a permanent glare, oozed grumpiness, and was probably a beast in bed. He'd never been Persephone's thing, but then she was one of many who'd shunned him because he was less than perfect.

Shallowness had been a protective shell, but it'd shattered with the vial of angel fire over her back.

His expression turned calculating. "Can I help you, Miss Nassim?"

"Persephone. I'm not hanging on formality like I used to." She rolled a shoulder and grimaced. She hadn't stood this long for months. Her bed was starting to seem like a better idea. Add in flying, and she was ready to drop into a puddle of smoldering nerves. No. She'd come too far. "I want to be a warrior."

It sounded absurd when she said it out loud. She folded her hands together, digging her fingers into her skin to keep them from twiddling.

To his credit, Director Vale didn't burst into laughter. He studied her for a moment. Was he deciding how to rebuff her now that he pitied her? But he said, "Follow me."

He swept up the steps to the door and held it open.

The stairs were easier to climb than flying, but she was trying not to obviously pant by the time she reached the top. Once inside, the director swung around her, leading her to another door. His office.

After they entered, he didn't go to the chair behind the desk. Instead, he pulled out one of the backless seats by a small table in the corner. "Sit."

She dropped, resisting the urge to whimper. Crawling into bed sounded like a dream right now.

"Why do you want to be a warrior?"

Direct, but he didn't look like the type for chitchat. "I want to give back to the realm."

His flat expression remained unwavering. "By hunting demons?"

She nodded.

"Why not a chaperone? A watcher?"

"I'm not snooping on humans."

As a chaperone, she'd wait by a dying human to lead their soul to the other side. Just wait to be useful. Hadn't she done enough of that?

As a watcher, she'd take notes on the goings-on in the human realm for analysts like Odessa. Smarter angels who could decipher patterns and determine whether one of the realms was in danger. The spying part got to her. She'd done enough of that before she was burned.

"I'm not a gossip." She bit her lip. "Anymore."

He cocked his head. "You haven't healed long enough to know what you are anymore."

The spoiled brat she thought she'd left behind reared her head. "I'm tired, okay?" All the things she wished she could tell her parents spewed from her mouth. "I'm so sick of being taken care of. Not because people really care— because, trust me, no one has been around to check on my well-being. My parents won't let me do a thing, and I'm even more useless than I was before.

"And while I get that I need to take responsibility, it's also really fucking hard when your own parents treat you like you can't tie your own robe. When they tell you how intelligent and refined and talented other kids are—like your mate and her sister—and you grow up watching your parents dote on others, giving them the respect you wish you deserved and can't figure out why you don't.

"And then, when my back almost got burned off, I saw how alone I was. How little anyone really cared. Only one person has been there for me, secretly checking on me when I wasn't being anyone else but me, and last night, I stayed awake all night and he didn't show.

"That's when I thought, Enough. *Enough.* I'm not a useless victim sitting around anymore. I've been a shit to warriors and they've been dicks to me, but you know, they were there for me when I needed them. I want to be that person for others. I want to be the one trying to prevent what happened to me from happening to another lost soul."

The director didn't move while she spilled her guts. Her face burned. How humiliating. She didn't know this male, and she'd been a classic bitch to his mate. Now she was practically pleading with him, begging him not to write her off like her parents did when he had no idea what she could do. The list of what she couldn't do would be too long to finish reading.

His wings twitched, and he sucked in a long breath. "I wouldn't take it easy on you because of who you are."

"I wouldn't expect you to."

"Or because of what you've been through."

She ground her teeth together. Warrior training wasn't held behind closed fences. She and the ones she'd thought were her friends used to sneak to the fences or fly overhead and watch the trainees. Mostly the males who trained with their shirts off.

Other than glistening muscles, she witnessed the sheer endurance they possessed. While she'd gotten to the director's office because of what she'd gone through, she wasn't sure she could stand again, much less train. "I'm weak."

"Physically, perhaps, but we can change that."

"Are you… Are you actually thinking of allowing me into training?"

"I have no problem letting you in, Persephone. The pain, the fatigue, the bruises will be your problem to deal with. You give my trainers too much attitude, and you're out. They don't think you can cut it, you're out."

Hope rose in her chest, masking some of the ache in her back. "I want to start right away."

"Your parents—"

"Are my problem."

She couldn't tell whether he smiled or grimaced. One side of his mouth didn't move much, thanks to the scars. "You're wrong there. When the children of senators don't do what their parents want them to do, there's hell to pay. I respect your parents, and your mother has been a valuable resource. I don't want to piss her off, but we will both face challenges with them. If they go to Senator Thomas, then I'll deal with him."

"Why would they go to Senator Thomas?" Could the old angel in charge of the senate forbid her from becoming a warrior? Why would he?

"They might think he could sway me."

"Fair." Refusing to let the momentum drop, she asked, "Can I start right away?"

Surprise rippled over his face, but a glint of respect shone in his eyes. "We'll get you a bunk, but I can't ignore your injuries."

Her heart hung heavy. She was already different. She would be coddled.

"Relax," he said, as if he could read her mind. "Running trainees into the ground without equipping them to be their best isn't good leadership. I happen to know what you went through, and I also know another female with similar injuries. After you're settled, you're going to meet with me. You'll go through orientation, and I'll see when you can meet with Felicia."

"No—"

"It's not your decision." He used the same tone he must use on an unruly recruit, which was what she was acting like.

Still, she couldn't let it go. "I'm not comfortable with Felicia."

"The problem with you and my mate and her sister is

how your parents treated them versus you. It's not with them. You need to decide for yourself what you think of them, just like you decided for yourself what you want to be when you grow up."

His words hit home. She was in charge of her life. For once. Her life was now a blank slate. A busted, taped-up slate, but hers. "Okay."

"*Yes, sir.*"

Her lips twitched. She'd never called anyone sir. "Yes, sir."

"Very well. Wait outside my office while I contact your future trainer and they arrange your bunk." When she rose, her legs shaking and the pain flashing, he said, "The person who was supposed to show last night… A warrior?"

Heat flamed her cheeks. "It was nothing. He'd just listen to my bad jokes to keep my mind off the pain."

"Bad jokes?" he said like he hadn't heard her correctly.

"What's the one place in the hospital where you can't hide?"

His brows drew together, and he shook his head.

"The ICU." And with that, she followed his orders and left his office.

URBAN CHECKED HIS PHONE. "What the hell?" he muttered as he read the message from Director Vale. He and Ransom had trolled Vegas all night, and now that it was lunchtime, the director beckoned them back to his office.

Ransom shrugged, affable as always. The search hadn't been terrible. Boring, yes. Unsuccessful, yes. But not bad. Ransom kept looking at Elodie's picture to the point Urban wondered if dads had spank banks. Technically, Ransom was a grandpa, and Urban wasn't used to working with warriors with families. Kids and shit. Ransom had all the muscles and reflexes of a warrior, but he was so damn nice.

Ransom gestured down the block. "There's an alley up ahead. We can ascend to the barracks."

Ascending was always the easiest part of transcending. They could return to their realm and not worry about vanishing and reappearing in front of a human. When they descended from Numen to the human realm, the factors to consider were more serious and the repercussions of fucking it up more severe. Revealing themselves to humans, accidentally or not, often cost an angel their wings.

They landed outside headquarters; Director Vale's office door was open.

Ransom knocked anyway.

"Come." Before they had a chance to sit in the chairs across from his desk, the director continued, "Ransom, Bronx and Harlowe are going to be working in Vegas with you."

Urban didn't want to be relieved yet. Was he getting a chance to work in Numen? He'd be able to make his nightly visits. "You need two to replace me?" It came off as a joke, but he was impatient for more information.

"No," Director Vale said. "This female is wilier than we thought. Jagger will be joining in the search tomorrow. Dionna will be taking charge."

"Almost like a team again." Urban missed the old days, almost regretted getting pulled, but a young, hurting female was waiting for him.

"Close, but I have another assignment for you." Director Vale eyed Ransom. "You can go. Get some rest, and Dionna will contact you with the address to the safe house Sierra set up in Henderson. You'll have to stay there until this Elodie is tracked down."

Urban adjusted his stance, his restlessness off the charts. He was usually a service dog, going where he was told, doing what he was ordered to do, humping when he could. His anxiety over the parameters of a mission was new and unwelcome.

Ransom shut the door when he left.

Director Vale folded his hands on his desk. "What's the only place in a hospital where you can't hide?"

"What?" Was he being stationed in a hospital? Was there another target roaming some clinic on Earth?

"The ICU."

The meaning dawned on him. Urban drew back, giving the director a questioning look. "You into dad jokes now?" The words left his mouth, and understanding yawned in his brain. Bryant Vale hadn't told a joke in his life. There was only one other reason he'd have one out of the blue. "How'd you find out?"

"You just confirmed it. But I had a visitor this morning, waiting for me when I got to work."

"Persephone was here?"

The director reclined in his seat. It wasn't going to be a quick discussion. "Face full of dirt and limping from a full-body pain that made my old aches flare up. She told me she respected a warrior who listened to her jokes, so she wants to be a warrior."

"She can't." She could barely walk. She'd been recovering for months.

"We'll see what she can and can't do." His eyes narrowed. "Why were you secretly checking on her?"

"Her parents wouldn't let me see her, even when I told them I was there when she was hurt. I helped her." They'd shooed him away like they would an annoying bug.

"That explains the secret part. Did you two have a thing?"

"No. Never." He'd been insulting to her when she'd hit on him. "I…wasn't the nicest to her before she got hurt."

"No one was. Because she wasn't nice either."

"She's changed."

"I'll say." He scrubbed his face. "Look, I don't know if she'll hack the training. I don't know if she'll turn back into the roving mean female we all knew, but she told me why she wanted to be a warrior, and I bloody well believed her." He threw his hands in the air. "If this experience goes tits up, I'll take the blame."

Persephone a warrior? Urban couldn't see it. Her smile was shy, the opposite of how she'd been before her attack. She liked bad jokes. Warriors saw some of the worst human behavior, and sometimes they couldn't stop it. Hiding their presence from humans took priority. If they couldn't yank a demon out of a human host and into the Mist to kill without witnesses, then they were stuck attempting to interfere with human methods.

And then there was the killing. Bloody. Gruesome. Demons didn't fight with honor.

Urban's worry for Persephone clawed up his throat. "She can't—"

"You're going to train her."

Urban's entire body jerked, which would've gotten him killed in the field. "Me?"

"Initially. Then she'll transition to train with the regular recruits." He spread his hands. "She's a special case. I'm not going to lie: She might be physically recovered, meaning her wounds are now scars, but she's not physically or mentally rehabilitated."

"Then why are you allowing it?" She'd lain in bed in pain and told jokes. She wasn't a warrior.

"Because I know how healing action can be. The feeling of being useful. And right now, that's the reason why her recovery's stagnated. She's stuck."

Urban pondered what the director had said and compared notes with his late-night discussions with Persephone. Her parents were smothering her, and she didn't feel like they were doing it because they cared about her. They didn't have faith in her abilities, in her competency. Persephone was becoming a prisoner in her own home. It was like her parents hated how she acted and figured this was a good way to keep her off the streets, so they reverted to the way things had been.

"Why did you pick me?"

"She trusts you. You wouldn't have been sneaking into her house if you agreed with how sequestered she's been. When her parents pound on my door and throw their senator status and all the things they've done for the warriors around, I can show them that I've assigned a special mentor to her. That she's getting special treatment. Perhaps you'll save me a bloody headache."

Urban wanted to jump at the chance. He didn't like the idea of one of the hard-asses in the training arena getting their hands on her. The director was right—she wasn't ready. But a sense of wrongness settled in his chest, and he needed a moment to figure out why.

"I agree, but…are we going through the motions? If she proves competent, is she going to get a fair shot at being a warrior?" He didn't care for that idea either. She'd been hurt enough, and it hadn't been thanks to demons. As a warrior, she'd be hunting the creatures from Daemon. The underworld. She'd be facing off with one or more in the Mist. Warriors were excellent fighters, but they could still get killed.

As a warrior, she'd have to wear vials of angel fire. The substance was one of the best weapons against demons.

Director Vale clasped his hands behind his head. His wings twitched as he considered the question. "Yes."

That was that.

Fists pounded on the door a second before it was rammed open. Urban jumped, ready to defend his boss. Director Vale's wings flared, but that was his only reaction.

Persephone's parents charged in.

"What's this about Persephone becoming a warrior?" Rage vibrated through Senator Nassim's body. His dark beard only made his brown eyes darker. The mass of black hair on his head was disheveled, like he'd been running his hands through it on the flight there.

"She's in training, yes," the director answered.

"No, she's not," Persephone's father said. "We need to get her home."

The director sat forward, looking every inch the male in charge. "She walked in here of her own accord, an adult, told me her reasons, and I've accepted her."

"Director Vale"—the senator spoke like the politician he was—"Persephone isn't in her right mind. She's been hurt, yes, but she was never mature enough to take on a duty for the realm."

"Massive angel-fire burns are life-changing." The director's steady gaze rested on the couple, challenging them to defy what he said while looking at his scars.

"I forbid it," her mother said.

"You cannot."

"I'll go to Senator Thomas," her father blustered.

"Try it. That bloody old male has started to annoy me with all his questions about how I run my position. I'd be happy to have it out with him." His gaze lifted to Urban. "You may go."

The senator's gaze brushed over Urban like it was the first time he'd noticed anyone else in the office. Not a hint of recognition lit his eyes. But he'd been next to his mate when he told Urban he had no business checking on their daughter.

Urban certainly had business now.

CHAPTER 3

The looks. She'd never gotten used to the looks. The prying eyes when she wandered through the realm. Like people couldn't figure out what the kid of senators was like. So Persephone had given them something to talk about. She'd earned all the catty remarks behind her back.

Shame burned her cheeks as she set her shoulders against the stares.

The barracks weren't separated by gender. They were large bays full of cots and wall lockers. A trunk that could slide under the bunk. The bathrooms weren't communal, thank the Almighty, but she'd be snoring among the rest of the new recruits.

A small blonde turned to her. "You're Persephone, right?" She wagged her finger over her shoulder. "The one who…"

The other recruits in the barracks held their collective breath. It was only afternoon, and most were out training. The ones inside were either between training sessions or recovering from injuries that took more than a snooze to heal.

Perhaps they weren't so different after all.

Wishful thinking. These recruits were nothing like her, and it wasn't something Persephone was proud of. "Yes. The burned back."

"Kadee. But your wings weren't hit? What happened again?"

It took a moment to register that Kadee was her name. "No. I was in the human realm." She reluctantly related the fake story her parents had come up with. Senator Colbert's treason had been covered up, and it stung like a saltshaker over her burns. "I went through the Mist and stumbled on a warrior and demon fighting. I got hit with a few drops. My wings were in their morph."

She wished she could tell the truth. About corrupt senators. About being taken advantage of. Of how she'd been in an office, on some compound in Florida, ready to spend her life with some male who might not give a shit but who seemed better than her bored life in Numen, and she'd been hit with a few stray drops. She was lucky she existed at all.

"Oof. At least there's that, huh? I see Senator Felicia once in a while with her broke-ass wings and—"

"Kadee." A male as young as Kadee, with wide, disbelieving eyes, nudged her. "You can't talk like that."

"Like what?" She threw her hands up. "Do demons care if I censor my speech?"

"Demons, no. The senator and others with injuries like hers?" He jutted his chin out like he was willing her to get what he was saying and shut up.

Their open speech was refreshing, and Persephone didn't mind that her injuries centered in the discussion.

Kadee propped her hands on her hips. Everyone was

dressed in black pants and shirts with heavy black boots. Persephone had changed into the same clothing after she was shown her bunk. Her lower lip was raw from biting down while she wrestled her shirt over her wings, but while it felt like a triumph to be so far removed from her normal, it was barely a beginning.

"Do you object to me calling your back broke ass?" Kadee asked, and the male's eyes widened farther. Another female pressed her fingers to her lips and closed her eyes. They all knew Persephone's parents were senators and she could complain to them and have the recruits booted from the program.

It made her want them to accept her more. But she wouldn't say yes and be needy. Wasn't that how she ended up being a bitch in the first place? Becoming what she thought they wanted hadn't served her well. "Well, my back's not broken, but the skin is all scarred, so maybe broke-ass skin?"

Kadee nodded like it made perfect sense. "See?" she said to the male.

"That's not the point," he grumbled. Then he turned his attention back to Persephone. "I'm McCall, but people call me Mac."

Kadee's lips twisted. "Trainer Stana calls you Butterfingers."

Mac's cheeks burned red. "It's a distraction technique."

The other female snickered. "Is that what you call dropping your daggers?"

"I don't know, is that what you call losing your balance when you kick something, Molly?"

Molly screwed her mouth up, and Mac rolled his gaze toward Persephone. "If you haven't pieced it together, we're the barracks of broken things."

The camaraderie among the three was something she'd

never experienced. Humor behind the ribbing, not meant to cut down but to equalize. No one in this group would be the mean girl ringleader.

Tension leaked from Persephone. "Then I'll fit right in."

"So you're seriously going to train?" Kadee asked.

The burn of the others' stares was back on her. "I am."

The heavy thud of boots sounded down the hall, and they all stared out the bay windows over the row of beds. Urban's scowling face came into view. Persephone's belly swirled and flipped like a human roller coaster.

She swallowed. What did he think of her plan? Did he believe she could do it? Did he even believe she was serious?

Unless he was here to tell her she was deluded and couldn't possibly start training, much less finish it.

His gaze collided with hers before he turned into the doorway. She swallowed. In her room in the dark, she couldn't see him well. Even when they faced each other, he was a mask of shadows. Big, strong shadows, but not as visible under the skylights that brightened the barracks.

His eyes were a lighter brown than she'd thought. Flecks of yellow she'd never noticed before were clear now. The heavy wings behind him were a darker gray. They'd shone with the ambient light from her window, but in the barracks, the color deepened.

However, those shoulders were as wide as she remembered. She'd seen him only a couple nights ago. But it felt like months, and maybe that was a closer description for how it felt seeing him now. The last time she'd talked to him before the attack and her recovery, she'd talked to him had been when he'd rebuffed her in the market. She knew what he looked like, but she'd been superficial then and her perusal had been the same.

"Nassim. Come with me." He spun on a heel. The recruits were standing rigidly, backs straight, wings held still, and hands by their sides.

"What? Why?"

This time Kadee's eyes flared. What had Persephone done to worry Kadee? An ominous cloud hung over her head.

"You're working with me."

She ignored the flutter in her stomach. The director had told her he wouldn't treat her differently. "But I'm with the broken things."

He cocked a brow and passed his gaze over the others. "At ease."

They relaxed, but Kadee curled her arms around herself. Mac stepped farther away from her, and Molly turned like she wasn't going to listen to every word.

"Director Vale assigned me to you. You need to catch up before you can join them."

Oh. It made sense, but she'd been ready to jump in with both feet and steel herself against the constant pain, which had lessened while she'd talked to the others. "What about—"

"Get your shit and get to the workout room. You have thirty seconds."

She drew back, but Urban marched away. What was that about?

"I can't believe you were talking back to him," Kadee hissed.

The girl who referred to everyone by their altered body parts couldn't believe Persephone's audacity? "Urban?"

"Yeah," Mac breathed. "Like, of all the warriors, you sass him?"

Oh, sass. Right. There was a rank structure. And she

was used to being at the top of all rank structures in Numen, thanks to her senator parents. It wasn't like anyone could know he'd lain next to her each night, laughing and whispering. "What do I need to bring with me?"

They all shrugged. The fear in their eyes was for her.

Ugh. She'd have to find out. She strode down the hall, the pull of gravity heavy on her scars. She hadn't stood this long for months and her stamina was at rock bottom, but she hadn't collapsed yet. She wouldn't have bet on herself this morning, though. It wasn't like she'd done more than roam the realm and look good before her injuries. Angels had natural healing ability, but it didn't build muscle.

"Shit." Where was the workout room? She had gone in the same direction as Urban. The hallway stretched to the end, where it went down a flight of stairs to the door. The bathrooms were behind her. Unless he sprinted, he had to still be on the floor.

Right before the stairs was a door with a *W* on it. Inside, Urban waited in the middle of the room with his arms crossed.

Awareness sizzled down her spine. The darkness of her bedroom had softened his edges. In the light of day, he was a deliciously hard man. His RBF—resting brooding face— had drawn her like a demon to an uncorrupted soul.

"Two seconds over." His voice was hard.

"I didn't know where the room was." She lifted her empty hands. "What was I supposed to bring?"

His right eye twitched. "Workout gear."

"Like?"

"For fuck's sake, Persephone, what the hell are you doing here?"

She recoiled. He stomped past her and closed the door.

Being shut into a room with him shouldn't have been a new experience, but this resonated like it was the first time. In reality, during their real first time alone together, she'd been in a fog of pain—and sad. So terribly sad and scared.

"Urban, I—"

"Why the hell did you march here and demand to be a warrior? You can barely stand. You're swaying on your feet right now."

Her lower lip stuck out. She could feel it. Trying to suck it in only made her mouth quiver. Tears burned at the backs of her eyelids, and while she'd cried plenty of times around him, that was a low she didn't want to reach. Crying right then would only prove them right, everyone who thought she couldn't do this.

"I am tired." She drew herself up, agony igniting around her shoulders. "But last night I realized I'm putting too much dependence on others."

He flinched. "I was on a mission."

The slight relief his admission gave her didn't change her stance. "The point is, I did nothing but wait. My days and nights revolve around people I'm dependent on. I don't want to be dependent anymore. I want to be the one they can lean on."

"And you picked now because I didn't show?"

When he put it like that, she sounded like an impulsive little girl. "I had time to think. I've had nothing but time to think, and centering my days on a visit from a male who feels obligated to check on me because he couldn't save me isn't exactly a healthy way to pass the time."

His scowl deepened. "Do you blame me for what happened?"

She was fully to blame, and she'd had plenty of time to

come to that conclusion. Juliette Colbert had had her talons sunk in at that point. Urban shunning her in the market might've been a spark, but Persephone had held the match and let it burn until she followed the senator to the human realm for some baseless mating arrangement. She'd been trying to fill the emptiness inside her. "I told you I don't."

He clenched his jaw and his gaze swung around the workout room. They stood in the open area with mirrors on one side and various equipment on the other. She didn't know what any of it was. If her life depended on it, she couldn't identify the stretchy bright-colored things hanging from the wall. They came from the human world. Everything did. She knew the basics of the human world but hadn't spent real time in the realm.

"How long have you been on your feet?"

Too long. "Since I got changed."

"You're tired?"

Ashamed, she still shook her head. He'd already pointed it out, so why ask? But she was determined to show some sort of strength.

"That's lesson number one. Be fucking honest with your team, or it can cost someone their life. Sit."

She glanced around. "Where?"

"The weight bench."

Her gaze jumped to all the metallic equipment. "The what?"

"Almighty," he said like a curse. "Second lesson—workout equipment."

While he walked around naming items, she stuffed her feelings down. As rudimentary as it was, she was training. She was actually doing it. The triumph would help when she had to acknowledge her nights with him in bed were over.

~

RANSOM HAD FOUND HER. He and the rest of the team working in Vegas with him had split up since they were only searching for Elodie. He refused to give up, needing to be the one who located her. Vegas wasn't his scene—he preferred snowy mountains and tall pine trees like when he visited his daughter—and it wasn't Elodie Rogers's either. She skittered through the old casino like there was a monster hiding behind each slot.

She'd braided her dark hair in twin braids that only made her stand out more instead of blend, but that was due to her ensemble more than the hair. She was dressed like she was a corn-fed Iowa girl and it was her first time in not just Vegas but any city. Canvas shoes with socks up to her knees, but pants ending just below the knee, and a billowy shirt with a cardigan thrown over top. She had a VIVA LAS VEGAS ball cap on her head with sunglasses resting on the brim.

Despite her raging tourist outfit, she was cute. Beautiful even, if one could see beyond her attire. She exhibited the ethereal quality a lot of Numen were unable to shake when they roamed Earth. It made her a target.

The demons playing the slots in their human hosts kept their attention on her like she was a beacon.

Ransom had never seen so many possessed human hosts in one spot. Sylphs were the lowest form of demon. Feral little creatures meant to disrupt a human's life and gather intel for the superior demons. Then there were symasters, the middlemen. They attached themselves to a human, invisible, and mucked up the person's day even more like the devil on the shoulder.

Archmasters were the...well, the masters. They could possess a host—control them and run around the human realm, creating havoc and enjoying themselves in the worst ways. The job of the sylphs and symasters was to make a human ripe for possession. And they'd been busy in this casino.

The hosts ran the gambit: young, old, vibrant and healthy, sucking on an oxygen tank, and the random server. These types of possessions made a warrior's job easy. Once the patron went to the restroom, a warrior could yank them to the Mist, the dewy realm between Numen and Earth, and no one would see them disappear.

Elodie stopped in front of a dime slot. She leaned in to peer at the pictures and giggled, like the images of apples and oranges and cherries delighted her more than a portrait hanging in an art shop.

His eyes drifted to her ass. She was petite but had curves that made his mouth water. How long had it been since he'd had sex? His dick reminded him, a long dang time.

He'd been so wrapped up in raising Sierra he hadn't dated. Before her mother had begged him to become her guardian and make sure Sierra's demon side was never discovered, he'd been one hundred and ten percent committed to his job.

After Sierra had grown and made his heart burst with pride when she became a warrior, he'd never wanted to be far away if she needed him. His commitment had been split between her and his job. A mate wasn't his priority. If he were injured severely he'd be matched with someone to share their healing abilities. If that happened, so be it. Otherwise, it had felt wrong to go out with someone— mess around, even—and hide such a huge part of his life. He didn't want to grow closer to someone while he was keeping them away from his daughter.

Then Sierra had fallen and he'd been a shell. But she was in a good place now, and her secret was more important than ever. Because he was the world's greatest grandpa.

He'd bought a shirt with that on it once after a visit to Sierra and her family. It'd gutted him to give it away before he'd returned to his home in Numen, but fallen angels were never supposed to be acknowledged again. His visits were the only times he ever broke the laws of his realm. Sierra was still a part of their team, and he bounced his grandson on his knee as often as he could.

So, yeah. The desire licking through his body was used to being suppressed. He did it automatically, but watching Elodie scamper to the restroom after an older woman made it harder to ignore. Until he got a good look at the human Elodie followed.

"Shit," he said under his breath. The archmaster possessing the human was clear as a bell, but if Elodie hadn't been trained to recognize a demon-possessed human, then she would be clueless and alone in close quarters with a demon. The creature would use his host to hurt the naive angel when they were alone. That was a temptation no demon could pass up.

Ransom needed to intervene. He wore simple blue jeans and a black T-shirt to blend better than Elodie, but walking into the ladies' room would be noticeable. Still, he couldn't let her stumble into danger.

She disappeared inside the restroom, and he wove through the rows of slots as quickly as he could. His heart rate kicked up. What were the chances the human host was taking a piss and wouldn't notice Elodie?

He took his phone out of his pocket and stared at the screen while he briskly walked across the casino floor.

Anxiety drove him as he pretended to be absorbed with the screen's contents and charged through the door.

Expecting to act as if he'd stepped into the wrong restroom, he looked up, feigning surprise, but he was really evaluating the situation. Frowning, he stared down the row of empty stalls. Labored breathing and low murmurs could be heard from the last stall, which was also the widest.

Cautiously, he stalked toward the door. It was latched, but when he looked down, stooping enough to see under the stalls, he saw two pairs of shoes. Elodie's and the host's. Alarm raced through him. Had Elodie been cornered? Was she hurt? He reached the door and yanked it open, the tiny metal bolt hopeless against his strength.

He could only blink. Elodie had cut off the woman's windpipe with her forearm, and she'd braced her feet to put all her weight into immobilizing the human. The human's irises had gone black, and her lips were peeled back in a sneer. Archmasters were the most powerful demons of the underworld, and this one was enraged. It would destroy the host in its attempt to overpower Elodie.

"What the hell are you doing?" Ransom yelled in a whisper. At this point, the human host was probably buried so deep in her own body she didn't know what was going on, but if Elodie crushed her windpipe, the angel would be the one in trouble.

Elodie's eyes narrowed, her face expressing hostility. "*You.*"

He recoiled. She knew him? "What are you doing?"

"Get out of here," she sneered.

This couldn't continue. She was risking her safety and her own wings if she continued what she was doing. The human could die, and Elodie would be declared a fallen angel. Or someone could walk in and Elodie could reveal their kind—she'd lose her wings for that too.

The words to yank the demon out of the host and into the Mist fell automatically from his lips as he reached for the older woman. Elodie tried to muscle him out of the way, but she was no match for his strength and the stall just wasn't wide enough for the three of them to move anywhere.

When the cool particles of the Mist surrounded him, he was already pulling a dagger from under his shirt. The demon whipped around, his yellow fangs bared. This one was smaller, and the curve to its back made it hard for it to fight. Ransom didn't have time to identify its gender, but it didn't matter. The demon had tampered with a human soul, and it was Ransom's job to make sure it never did it again.

He plunged the blade into the demon's abdomen. The demon punched out with his talon-tipped hands, but Ransom ducked and spun, stabbing the thing. The creature tried again. Ransom plunged the blade into it. Over and over, he wore the demon down until it collapsed. Yanking the vial of angel fire from under his collar, he was about to uncap it and end the demon forever when Elodie attached herself to his arm.

She'd followed them?

"Whoa!" he yelled, juggling the vial. He hadn't uncapped it, or they'd both be nursing permanent angel-fire wounds. "What are you—"

But she was at the demon's side. "Tell me what I want to know, and I'll spare you."

She'd do what now? "Elodie."

She poked the demon in one of the stab wounds. "Tell me everything you know."

The demon's milky eyes glared, baneful. "Ask the protector of a half demon."

Ransom didn't think. He uncapped the vial of angel fire and tipped it onto the demon, starting with the head. The creature didn't have time to scream.

Elodie jumped up and pushed Ransom in the chest. "Stop!" She stared down at the smoldering demon, her eyes wide, frantic. The head had already burned off. She rounded on Ransom again. "You lying bastard."

"I'm not a liar." He didn't always tell the whole story, but he avoided lying if at all possible.

"Why would the demon call you a protector of a half demon?"

Technically, Ransom protected two half demons from being discovered by the Numen population. The senate knew about Sandeen but not Sierra's secret. Only her warrior team and the director held that knowledge. "He's a demon. He lies."

"So does our leadership." Her amber eyes flashed. "So do all the senators. And so do you."

"What are you doing, Elodie?"

She drew herself up to her full height, still a foot shorter than him. "Our realm doesn't have journalists. There's no flow of information, which I'm sure you're acutely aware of."

"The senate releases what they need everyone to know." Half demons and the senate's trade agreement with Daemon was not one of those things. Senator Thomas was tight-fisted when it came to the senate's dealings as it was. Wrongdoings didn't leave the senate coliseum.

"They release only what's beneficial for them. Our realm has been under attack, and we're all clueless, but a lot of our residents have been victims."

How did she know? He still tried to argue. "The realm

is safer than ever—and it's been kept that way since the dawn of time."

She scoffed, hands on her hips, and toed the demon slowly dissolving into the ground through the thick, damp grass. There was nothing in the realm but grass and mist. "But it's not. I have it on good authority that a half demon has been in Numen. That should be impossible."

He needed an answer from her. Perhaps being obtuse would get her to talk. "Wouldn't the half demon also be half angel?"

Her eyes narrowed. "I knew it."

"I'm speaking theoretically."

She shook her head. "No. You're going to have to kill me, too, if you don't want me to find out what's going on."

"Elodie." He was going to tell her she was being unreasonable, which would be a barefaced lie. She was tap-dancing on the truth, and he needed to know how she knew, exactly what she knew, and why. But what she said sank in. "What do you mean, kill you *too*?"

Her lower lip wavered. "My boyfriend."

"Who is?"

"Don't pretend you don't know the story."

He shrugged helplessly. The last hour had been confusing. "I was sent after you because you're putting yourself in danger, snooping around the fallen angel's old club."

"He's dead too, isn't he?"

"You seem to be the one with the information." Jameson was dead. Andy was dead. Elodie was observant enough to realize they were gone and had been dealt with by Numen. Did she know Jameson had died saving his son, Ransom's teammate, Jagger? Worse, did she know Jameson had been able to cross into Numen to save his son? Something that should've been impossible and was kept from the general

Numen public. The existence of fallen angels was supposed to be forgotten by everyone. Jameson's story would only give loved ones ideas for their fallen. The information could give them nefarious ideas, which was why the story had been suppressed. "Who was your boyfriend?"

She made a disgusted sound. "Senator Thomas's grandson?" When he shook his head, she rolled her eyes, but he caught the flash of grief. "Tommy was killed six months ago in the human realm."

Ransom had heard about the senator's grandson, a fairly young male who'd been born to parents centuries old. Just like everything else, Tommy's grandfather, Senator Thomas, kept his private and personal business under wraps. If Ransom stopped to think about it, it was shocking the Numen knew so little of their staid leader.

The shock of Tommy's death had rippled through the realm, but he'd assumed the cause was why it'd been suppressed. The story was that he'd fucked with a possessed sex worker who'd gotten hold of some angel fire. "I'm sorry."

She shoved a finger into his shoulder. "You should be, but not because of why you think. They lied. That bullshit story getting spread around the realm is just that. Tommy and I had just started dating, and not once did he ever have to pay for sex."

He tried to fit together all the pieces, but he was left with a heap of useless facts. "I don't get it."

"He heard his grandfather talking. He told me what he knew, and then he ended up dead. Get it now?"

Shit.

Shit.

The warriors involved were all under orders to keep what had gone on for the last few years quiet, but under no circumstances should they kill their own to keep the secret.

"Yeah," she said, disgust dripping from her tone. "You get it now. I know it all. That half demon you apparently protect. The trade between our realm—the real reason the so-called prostitute had a vial of angel fire. And you're on the team Director Vale used to lead. You're all in on it. And I'm going to blow the story wide."

The half demon Elodie knew about was Sandeen. She didn't know it, but she threatened his daughter's and grandson's safe existence. His daughter had suffered for something she had no control over. He couldn't let her get hurt again, and he'd sever his own limb before anyone brought danger to his grandson's doorstep. "Elodie."

She jumped back, suddenly pale. Her gaze darted around, and when she took another step, he knew she would disappear from the realm. He'd have to start all over again looking for her. Meanwhile, she'd be more determined than ever, and she'd know to start investigating his life.

He lunged for her, his fingers curling around the band of the fanny pack at her waist. When she stepped out of the realm and onto the dark lawn of a small house in Numen, he was right there with her.

When she spun on him, her mouth opened, a scream beginning to erupt. He clamped a hand over her mouth. She tried to spin out of his grip, but he yanked her to himself, banded an arm around her waist while keeping her mouth covered, and looked around.

"Sorry. I'm sorry." He'd made a mess. Her scream built against his hand. "I'm not going to hurt you."

She struggled more, but he held her tighter.

"Listen—I'm not going to hurt you. I swear." How he kept his word when he was cutting off any sound and keeping her from fleeing, he didn't know. One problem at a time.

She kicked at his shins.

"Dammit, I'm not going to hurt you. But if you keep doing what you're doing, you're going to get killed. You don't know everything, and it's made you a giant target."

Her flailing didn't quit, but she was either tiring or was listening to his warnings.

He looked around. The house had to be a safe spot for her. It was the first place she had instinctively run to. "Is this your house?" he growled into her ear, absolutely hating the position he was in.

Her feet were off the ground, and she kicked his shins.

As if she would feel safe with him when someone close to her had been killed for knowing what she knew and he wasn't letting her go free. He needed to get them inside.

He marched to the house, his footsteps lurching, thanks to her assault. A high-pitched whine left her. She refused to give up trying to scream. He hip checked the door open, and the flimsy lock broke easily enough. Breaking and entering wasn't a problem in the angelic realm.

The lights came on automatically. He appreciated being able to see, but if any of Elodie's neighbors looked through the windows, they'd find a warrior accosting her. Making his way to an interior room, he found a small office. A tiny office. But he was creative and could find a way to secure her. Then he'd notify his team he had her position and figure out what the hell he was going to do.

She was a threat to his team. But the story she'd told meant there was still trouble within the realm. Her boyfriend was the head senator's grandson, and he'd known more than he should. And now he was dead. She would be, too, if Ransom let her go. Then his family would be in danger, and he couldn't allow it. So he'd have to sit on

Elodie until she agreed to either shut up, cooperate, or both.

He'd hate himself the whole time. Even more, because each time she struggled, he couldn't ignore her lush ass wiggling against him. For a guy who'd spent his life being a good male for his realm and then for his daughter, he became a bastard quickly enough.

CHAPTER 4

$\mathcal{U}$rban was early to training. He'd hardly been able to sleep all night. Thoughts of Persephone and how she hadn't even known what a damn weight bench was floated through his mind. She'd been sheltered, even for a Numen, and the way she'd looked like she was ready to drop when he was talking to her tore at his heart.

Spending the night wishing he lay next to her in bed, telling jokes and softly laughing, didn't help either. He had one, a joke he'd meant to share the other night when he'd been called away.

Persephone trudged in, blinking and biting back a yawn. Her wings were stiff, and her clothing was haphazard, like she'd tossed them on and promptly forgotten about them. This wasn't the Persephone the rest of the realm knew. Even though it'd been months since the incident, other Numen would still be expecting her to be walking perfection and streaming insults. They had no idea that female had been burned away.

Who was she now? Did she even know? He'd start helping her figure it out by trying to forget about how he wanted to ask how she slept. Had her parents gotten through Director Vale and had she fought with them?

For now, she had to be like every other recruit. "The attention you pay to the detail in your clothing reflects on how well you function in the field."

She crinkled her brow and pursed her lips like she was trying to decipher what he said.

"Your clothing. Straighten your shirt and tuck it into your sweats."

Understanding dawned, lightening her dark-brown irises. She tugged at the hem of her top, wincing as she did so.

"Sore today?" He shouldn't be asking. She needed to handle her emotions by herself.

"Yes. You'd think our healing would tackle stiffness better, but the mornings are the worst."

Her body was working overtime. She'd likely be healing her scarred area every day of her life. The thought tugged at his heart and that had to be why he blurted, "Two sticks walked into a bar. The third one ducked."

She considered it, a furrow lining her brow. "That one's awful. Why do bees have sticky hair?"

"Because they use a honeycomb."

She finished tucking her shirt in, her shoulders stiff, but she was looking stronger than yesterday. "You heard that one already?"

He'd planned to use it later this week. "Okay, let's get started. Grab a band."

A moment of alarm coursed through her gaze, but she glanced at the multicolored bands on the wall. Satisfaction filled her expression.

Good God. She was afraid she wouldn't remember what a band was? This girl's uncertainty had driven her to be someone else, and after the attack, she was almost worse than before.

Because she'd figured out how to be a bitch. She didn't know how to be herself. When others questioned her before her injuries, deep down, she knew they weren't talking to the real her. But now she was open, vulnerable, and she was defaulting to insecurity.

He'd worked with cocky warriors his whole life, egos the size of the realm. How was he going to build her up to train with recruits who'd love to tear her down and make themselves better?

He had to treat her like other recruits. "Run through the stretches I showed you yesterday."

There it was again. The hesitancy.

This wouldn't do. She wasn't a normal recruit, or his ass wouldn't be personally working with her. "And with each change in pose, I want you to repeat to yourself these five things."

She nodded and stretched the band between her hands to limber up her shoulders.

"I'm funny, and I don't care what anyone thinks."

Her eyes widened. "What?"

"Do it."

"I'm funny and—No, this is—"

"Do it."

Disgruntled, she finished the phrase and changed the position of her arms so one was shoulder height and the other was down. He had to get her used to raising her arms above her head, and that'd take working on making the scar tissue pliant.

She'd hate this one. "I'm going to be a strong fucking warrior."

She wrinkled her nose but said it and then switched arms.

"Say it." When she uttered it under her breath, he said, "Next is I'm smart." She shook her head, and he snapped, "Do it."

"I'm smart," she huffed.

"I want you to repeat that one ten more times."

She dropped her arms. "What's this about, Urban?"

He ticked a finger up. "One, this'll help you learn to quit questioning me. I'm only going to get more strict and your real trainer will be ruthless." He raised another finger. "Two, you need to strengthen your mind as much as your body, and it starts with how you think about yourself."

Her lower jaw worked, and shame crept back into her expression.

Not on his watch. He crossed to her, doing something he'd never do with another recruit. He stood close to her, closer than was appropriate, and lifted her chin with two fingers. It was the first time he'd really touched her beyond hauling her back to Numen to heal. In her bed, they'd kept to their respective sides. "You have a sense of yourself you've ignored too long. And if you build it up, the bullshit anyone else says can't get through. You got me?"

She nodded, but her doubt didn't vanish.

He didn't want to take his fingers off her warm skin. "I happen to think you're pretty amazing. Strong as hell and resilient. Those are good warrior traits."

Her eyes widened, and she whispered, "Really?"

"Really. I didn't like the Persephone from before." Hurt simmered in her eyes, but he continued. "I thought she was fucking hot but not likable." He ducked his head to make sure she couldn't break eye contact. "Just like you intended. You made her that way. You got everyone to treat you just the way you wanted. If you can do that with a fake Persephone, why can't you do that with the real one?"

"Because they didn't need to like the fake Persephone."

"Lesson number three, Percy." The nickname slipped out, and he liked it too much. Not the name itself, but how it meant there was something more between them than jokes and stretches. "Why do you give a fuck who likes you or not?"

He let her go and stepped back before he crossed further over the line. "Work on answering that question as you finish going through the stretches. And repeat every mantra."

Why do you give a fuck who likes you or not?

Persephone tried to come up with an answer, but she didn't know. She wanted to be accepted, but why?

Because her parents didn't accept her? She wasn't the kid they wanted.

But she was the kid they had, and maybe…they could just deal with it.

Once she had come to that realization, the mantras Urban had assigned her came easier.

I'm funny, and I don't care what anyone thinks.

I'm going to be a strong fucking warrior.

I'm smart.

And the last two he'd added to make it five.

I don't give a fuck who likes me or not.

I am a badass.

The day of training had gone well. She worked on strength and range of motion with her back and overall mobility—and she suspected some of the exercises were meant to build confidence.

She'd never get used to having Urban's attention on her. Visiting in the dark was different from when he watched her move, his focus on her mind and body. She'd thrived on being visible before. Being publicly problematic. But one male's scrutiny and her balance suffered—inside and out.

She was finishing her stretches. "I think I can move my arms farther than yesterday."

From her position, with one hand curved over her head while she leaned to her right side with her wings in a neutral position, she could see only Urban's boots. He made her rotate her head from oriented toward the floor to the ceiling.

"That's the goal. Up."

She changed positions to look at the plain white ceiling. The tiny spots of scar tissue around her neck pulled and sparked with pain, but she was growing used to the movement. "It's weird, though. I thought once I healed, that was it. I was healed."

"The director swears that when he keeps moving, he feels better. And… Oh, hey."

She frowned and straightened. Felicia had wandered into the training center. Her gaze landed on Persephone but lacked interest.

Self-conscious, Persephone folded her arms, trying not to look like she was hugging herself. What was Felicia doing there?

Urban wandered toward the door. The look he shot Persephone was almost apologetic. "Felicia's going to talk to you for the last hour. Director Vale's orders."

"About what?" But she knew. She'd hoped the director had dropped the subject. She wasn't as defensive around Felicia as her sister, Odessa. Her mother adored the Montclaire sisters, but Odessa was her doll and the one Persephone had been the most horrible to. Felicia had always scared Persephone. She was harder. More blunt. Didn't give a shit what anyone thought. Felicia was everything Persephone couldn't be, and Persephone had assumed Felicia was also everything her mother wanted.

Urban disappeared, and Persephone scowled at the door he closed.

"Well. I can see you're thrilled." Felicia's tone was rueful. Persephone couldn't detect hostility, but the female had started as a senator's daughter and was now a senator herself. She could be anything she damn well wanted, and Persephone had learned to tread carefully around that high-society crowd.

"It depends." Persephone rolled her shoulders. It was only her second day of training. She was getting used to standing, but she was weary. Her wings were growing heavier the longer she stood. Her gaze drifted along Felicia's uneven wings. There were spots where feathers didn't grow. Bony knobs where smooth bones should be. But they were out and held high. "What are you going to tell me?"

"I don't have to tell you that people will be shitty to you, but then you also look like nothing's wrong, so maybe you'll be fine."

Compared to Felicia, Persephone's appearance looked fine, but she doubted anyone would see her and think she was okay. She clenched her jaw. "I'm well aware of how shitty people can be."

"I'm sure you are," Felicia mused, scrutiny narrowing her eyes.

Persephone's patience snapped. She had no right to be angry, but she was. She'd earned what everyone thought of her. She'd worked hard to make them dislike her but also to respect her. No one wanted to be insulted, and Persephone had had a lifetime of it. "I get it, okay. I was an awful person. Is that what you're here to point out? To tell me that I'll be the target now that I'm injured?"

Slight confusion marred Felicia's brow. "Didn't you hear how I used to behave?"

"I don't know what you're talking about. I told everyone that you sleep around and that you were responsible for breaking up Jagger and the female he was going to mate."

Instead of looking angry, the corner of Felicia's mouth tipped up. "Oh, that. Yeah, I know you did, but you didn't start it, and you weren't the only one who kept it going. The only time I was really salty about you was when you were supposed to mate Jagger when he was acting as my bodyguard."

Persephone snapped her mouth shut. This wasn't going how she expected the discussion to go. "I didn't want to, for the record." Feeling like she was sold off like a problem heifer was what had landed her in Florida, burning.

"I didn't either," Felicia said. "For the record."

"Didn't what?"

"Break up Jagger and what's-her-name."

Persephone's lips twitched. She had a feeling Felicia knew the female's name. "Okay?"

"Right. I was a raging bitch to him—and to most people. Hurt people often lash out the worst."

Persephone lifted her chin. "I'm sorry. For what I said. For being an asshole to Odessa. And for what happened to you."

"I'm not Odessa, and I can't accept an apology for her." Felicia's blue eyes darkened. "It sucks, doesn't it? And when the people responsible are dead, what do you do?"

"What do you do?" She wasn't asking rhetorically, but she hadn't thought that much about it until Felicia said it. Now she couldn't not focus on it. There was an anger that had nowhere to go. She was so fucking furious, but the people who'd done this to her were dead. The people who'd driven her to that point were very much alive, however; they should've been the two people in her life she was closest to.

"I live each day grateful for what I have." When Persephone's wings dropped, Felicia continued. "I know. Trite, right? But it's really all you can do. We aren't exempt from the stages of grief, and sometimes you just cycle through them. Sometimes you're at acceptance for years and then one day… You're so damn angry. And then you have a choice. Do you stay there, or do you look around at what you have and think how bad it could've been?"

She mulled over what the other female had said. She didn't know what happened to Felicia, but she'd heard her parents talking about an attack on the sisters when they were teens. After school, Felicia spent most of her time in the human realm, and when she was in Numen, she'd kept her broken wings morphed. "I'm cycling through the stages at warp speed, but I don't think I'm staying at acceptance very long."

"I know. I've been there." She looked toward the workout benches. "Want to sit?"

"Do I look that bad?"

"You're listing to the side."

Persephone winced. She'd gone from being totally secluded to revealing her weaknesses to anyone who was around. She shuffled to a bench and sat, sighing as the floor took the weight of her wings. "How do you do it?"

Felicia sat on another bench. "Jagger worked with me a lot. For a while, we thought maybe I could fly again, but they just aren't aerodynamic anymore."

"That sucks."

Loss registered in her expression. "Yeah, it does. But Jagger takes me with him. It's not the same, but it's not a complete loss. But the director's right—the more you move, the easier it gets. I know we think we're healed and we're done. And while no Numen has really studied angel-fire burns, I think it's like how we can get rough hands."

Rough hands? She thought of Urban's raspy fingertips when he touched her chin. She'd dated males before, guys like her, raised in privilege. Soft. It wasn't like they lacked muscles, but it seemed they dipped themselves in vats of salve every night. "Calluses."

"Constant friction. Our healing abilities are limited, and at some point, I think our bodies decide how much energy to spare on repetitive injuries. So I'm thinking it's reversed. We healed ourselves. Bare minimum. But we have to keep telling our bodies that no, there's more that can be done. More range of motion. More pliable scar tissue. Less pain with movement. We'll never be one hundred percent, but I can turn a fifty percent into a sixty percent."

Persephone nodded. "Makes sense." It wasn't the information. She liked talking to Felicia like this. Like they were equals and Persephone didn't have to think about how she wasn't like the Montclaire sisters and therefore was a failure. "Is that what the director and Urban wanted you to talk to me about?"

"I don't know. I think so. It's not like Bryant is going to open up a lot about when he was hurt. You're here, and that says enough about what he thinks. And there's the old director."

"Leo Richter."

"Yep. He's been doing really well, but he fell into quite the pit of despair for a while. And that's the thing—people won't pull you out. Not a Numen. It's got to come from within you. Our race is too vain to pull someone with disfiguring injuries back from the brink."

Harsh but true. Numen were vain. Their healing ability

only added to it. And for a while, that had been Persephone's concern. She could hide the scars on her back, but sometimes…

Sometimes she wanted to show them the hell off. She'd earned them by being trusting, and that was an awful way to get hurt.

"So, anyway." Felicia rose. "I'm around if you want to talk. Your mother is quite upset, by the way."

"I'm sure she told everyone what a fool I am." The bitterness that escaped wasn't intentional, but it hung in the air like a thick cloud.

Felicia looked at Persephone like she saw right through her. "Senators are a different sort. I can't speak on parental issues—I certainly had my own—but I'm around if you want to talk."

She left, and Persephone was stuck in her thoughts.

Urban entered and closed the door. "How'd it go?"

"How were you and the director expecting it to go?"

His gaze shuttered. "It's not like we have a blueprint of how to deal with you."

She recoiled. "Deal with me?"

"Didn't it go well? Did she say something?"

"No. Yes—I mean, it went fine. But being ambushed by a talk from the female that my parents want me to be like is something I'd like a heads-up about."

"You're in training—and Director Vale did tell you. Otherwise, we don't owe you a heads-up. If we think it'll make you stronger and benefit you, we'll do it."

He'd do it. The complete control and arrogance he spoke with infuriated her—but also sent a curl of delight through her belly. Like she wanted to stand up and purr, *What else do you want me to do?*

She stood, but she wasn't submitting. "I'm tired of people who think they know what I need. What I should do. How I should act." Her anger was irrational. She blamed the fatigue and not getting her nights alone with Urban anymore.

"Then warrior training may not be for you."

She sucked in a breath. "You don't think I can do it."

He shook his head, keeping his expression unreadable. "No, I didn't say that. But you're already getting away with a lot. You're getting special treatment, and dammit, when you're not with me, then what? You going to throw a tantrum and try to get your way?"

"How dare you!"

He crossed to her so fast she flinched. "I dare because I'm your trainer. I dare because Stana out there"—he shoved a finger toward the second-story window—"won't care if she stomps you into the ground. She only cares if you can get back up. I dare because demons won't care if you're offended. They'll rape you and then murder you— or vice versa. You'll need to react to stay alive. No doubts. No hesitation. And if you can't tolerate me not doting on you to get you ready, then you need to walk right out that door."

Her hurt and indignation rose with each word that left his mouth. But then she saw it. When he said demon, the worry was visible. The stark concern buried in his dark eyes. She would've missed it if he wasn't standing so close.

She swallowed her feelings. Because the rest of what he said was true too. She was getting special treatment because she needed it. The director, Urban, and even Felicia weren't like her parents. They were genuinely trying to help her.

Her emotions were her own to control. So she chose a different response. "I'm afraid for calendars."

His scowl was instant. "Why?"

"Their days are numbered."

His confusion deepened, turning to disbelief. "Did you just make a fucking joke?"

She shrugged.

"Hell, Percy." He curled his hand over her cheek and dropped his head.

When his lips touched hers, she froze. How often had she imagined this? How much had she silently cut off the fantasy before it started? He'd stuck around out of guilt.

But he was kissing her. And she was marginally sure he wasn't supposed to.

Then she let go. Because he was kissing her. His lips were soft but firm, and the scrape of his stubble hit around the sensitive skin of her lips.

She moaned. It'd been months since she'd been touched, and none of the males she'd been with before had been this…masculine. There were no clogging scents from bath soaps or essential oils, but leather oil and soap. The combination shouldn't work, but it did.

His hot tongue licked across her bottom lip, and she opened, ready to feel him inside her mouth.

"I don't care if she's training, I want to talk to her." A voice in the hallway broke through the building haze of lust.

Urban jumped away so fast a cold draft slapped her across the face. She was blinking at the vivid blue sky through the window when the door banged open and her mother shouted, "Persephone. Come!"

The kiss had been over so fast she doubted it had happened. "I'm not a dog," she said without thinking. Her mother had barged in on them, but Persephone stuck to her response, grateful that the intrusion helped her forget she'd just had her lips on Urban's.

She turned to face her angry mother, lifting her wings as much as possible to look as strong as she could.

Mother's expression turned to granite. "Don't speak to me like that."

Maybe it was the way Urban's kiss had left her stunned, but she couldn't keep her mouth shut. "Like what? Like how you talk to me?"

Her mother's inhale was audible. "Come with me. You're done here."

"No, I'm not."

There was a pause before her mother looked from her to Urban. "What was going on here before I arrived?"

Urban didn't flinch, but Persephone's heart was pounding. She'd never been so afraid to be busted with a guy, not even when she was a teen and kissing males in the market.

This kiss had been personal, and she couldn't have anyone else find out. "We were training. That's what I'm here for."

"You're not a warrior," her mother said with a scoff.

That was it. "I'm not Odessa Montclaire either, but that never stopped you from wishing I was." Her mother looked at her like she didn't know what she was talking about. "And I'm over it, Mother. I'm over the way you and Father hid me away because you're so ashamed of how I turned out. Well, it's not your choice. I let how you felt about me affect me long enough. I changed myself for it. I'm here. And I'm going to be a warrior." She squared her shoulders with confidence she didn't feel.

"Persephone." Mother's tone was hard to identify. Hurt? Disbelief? Was she stunned?

"You know what? They're being really considerate about my injuries, and they don't have to. But you know why they're doing it? So I can be the best warrior possible. They aren't trying to run me off. They didn't write me off as soon as I walked through the door. That's more than my own parents did for me."

"We didn't—"

"You did. And I'm done. You can throw my things on the lawn. I'll get what I need here." She stormed past her mother, grateful for the few minutes she'd had to sit and rest her back. Because when she breezed down the hall, she kept her wings high and proud—and for the first time, the pride was real.

CHAPTER 5

This wouldn't do.

Ransom scrubbed his face. Elodie was still sleeping. The office hadn't worked. She would've been secured on the hard floor with her head shoved into the foot of a desk. So he'd tied her to her bed, regretting the red marks digging into her soft skin. What kind of bastard noticed how soft his captive's skin was when he was binding her up in her own house?

What kind of ass noticed how she smelled like fresh rain on a field of blooming wildflowers?

But she had fallen asleep faster than he'd expected, and she'd continued sleeping. She must've run herself ragged in her search for answers. Perhaps she'd been on the run, in hiding, or watching over her shoulder, and subconsciously she knew Ransom wouldn't hurt her and would protect her, so she slumbered like the dead.

Was that wishful thinking from a guy who had guilt gnawing at his organs?

While she was passed out, he'd had plenty of time to doze on the floor of her room. It was no less than he deserved. When he was awake, he was bombarded with thoughts. What in the world had he gotten himself into?

He couldn't keep her hostage.

He couldn't hurt her. But he had to keep his family safe.

She woke with a whimper. "My arms," she murmured.

He rolled up and was by her side in an instant. "I'm sorry about that. It's…temporary?"

Her eyes blinked open, but it took a second for full recognition to hit her. Then she gasped. "You tied me up!"

He winced. "I'm sorry."

"You keep apologizing, but I'm still tied up."

"Yeah." He stroked his gaze down her body. "About that."

Pink bloomed on her cheeks. "Pervert."

"What? No, I was trying to figure out—" He groaned and let out a sigh. "Look. I don't want to do this, and I don't want you to get hurt, so I—"

There was a knock on the door. Instead of hope that someone would discover she'd been captured, fear lit her brown eyes. She held her breath, and her gaze darted from him to the door of her bedroom.

"It's Director Vale. I didn't know what to do, so I called him."

"He'll kill me. I know all the secrets he's been keeping."

"No. He doesn't kill innocents. And you, Elodie, are innocent. You are ours to protect as much as any human."

Her lips parted. Tears shimmered in her eyes. "You lie."

"It'd have been easy to kill you and blame the demons you were chasing."

She swallowed hard but finally nodded.

Another knock, harder this time. "I'll be right back."

The director looked as disgruntled as ever. Odessa was with him and gave Ransom a small wave.

"Thanks for coming." He led them to the bedroom.

Elodie was glaring at the ceiling, but the quick rise and fall of her chest betrayed her terror.

"Oh my gosh, Elodie. How are you?" Odessa sat on the side of the bed. "Oh, gosh." She rested her hand on Elodie's forearm. "We're going to help you. I know it doesn't look like it, but that's what we're here for. There are a lot of factors, and that's why Ransom…"

Tied her up.

"Tell me about the young male who was killed," Director Vale said, his voice soft but impatient. Ransom wished the guy could be a little less abrupt.

Elodie's frantic gaze darted from the director to Odessa and darkened when it landed on Ransom.

"We're not going to hurt you." How often could he tell her that while she was tied up before she thought he was as evil as a demon?

She kept her gaze on him for several moments. Deliberation took its place in her eyes. "He knew everything, and they killed him," she finally said before repeating everything she'd told Ransom. Director Vale's jaw hardened as she talked about Sandeen, and Odessa paled. "So there it is. You're going to kill me now."

"No," the director said quietly. "We're not." He ran his tongue across his teeth before he spoke again. "Do you realize the panic it could cause if all this got out?"

"Do you realize the death and destruction it's causing now?" she shot back.

Ransom chewed his cheek, willing her to be quiet, to forget everything she'd heard, but that was wrong. Elodie was her own person, and right now she was the voice of the Numen general public.

"We're doing the best we can for the realm," the director said. "Sandeen is an asset."

"He's a half demon who can enter the realm," Elodie

said flatly. "I think it's important we know what we might come face-to-face with within the bounds of the realm. If there's one, there's more."

Odessa blinked like she was trying not to look at Ransom. Director Vale remained unflinching, but Ransom drew in a quick breath.

"I'd like her to meet Sierra." The wild thought he hadn't acknowledged was out of his mouth, and he couldn't take it back.

"Ransom," Odessa said, her voice full of concern. "You can't think…"

"I'll have to talk to her, but I think, maybe in this case… things need to change." As long as Sierra had to be in hiding, that meant she was in danger. The low-grade anxiety Ransom lived with would always be a constant. He'd always be worried, but maybe… Maybe the truth could set his daughter and her family free.

"Why Sierra?" Elodie was sharp. "She's fallen. You're not supposed to know where she is."

He'd slipped. Sierra was fallen, but she hadn't had to suffer long after her wings were taken. He tipped his head and thought about what he'd say. Before he spoke, he gave Director Vale a deliberate look. "I think that needs to change too. And I think you can help me, but once we go down this path…I can't allow you to be a threat to her."

Elodie shook her head. "How can I be a threat? She's fallen. She should be rotting in a ditch."

"Abso-fucking-lutely not," he snarled, and her eyes widened. "You don't know what she's gone through or what she's done for this realm."

"No, I don't," Elodie said, her defiance strong despite still being bound. "But I imagine all the others whose loved ones have lost their wings would be interested in how you seem to know about your daughter while they had to cut an entire person out of their lives."

Odessa straightened, smoothing her hands over her pristine white robes. Her nervous gaze darted to her mate, but the director was studying Ransom.

"I agree," the director said, and Ransom's eyes widened, his lips twitching. "Surprised? I've acted out of necessity, but it'd be nice to be proactive for a change. Besides," he growled, "I don't trust ninety percent of those fucking senators, and the ones I do trust annoy the shit out of me." His gaze flicked to his mate. "Except Felicia, of course."

Odessa's smile was indulgent, like she knew her mate was full of it. "Of course."

"Fine. Talk to Sierra. Work with Elodie. Come up with a plan." The director eyed Elodie. "You good with that?"

She glared at all of them. "Do I have a choice?"

"Do you want our help?" Ransom asked, annoyed. This female didn't know what she was walking into or what they were trusting her with. What he was trusting her with. His world.

His whole damn world.

"All right. I've got a bloody headache brewing at the barracks, so you're in charge of this mess, Ransom." With that, the director and Odessa left.

Elodie's mouth was set in a stubborn line. Ransom pinched the bridge of his nose. "I'm going to make that call."

"Are you going to untie me first?"

Tying her up had done unspeakable things to him. Made him feel inappropriate in unlimited ways. Putting his hands on her satiny skin wouldn't help to suppress those thoughts. And he didn't want trouble now that she knew he was in contact with his daughter.

"When I come back, I'll let you go and we'll eat, but I really need to call Sierra."

"I can't believe you're still talking to her."

The look he gave was heavy. "If you had a child and they needed help even though they'd done something unthinkable, would you let them suffer? Would you be willing to forget them? Maybe the other families of fallen are stronger than me. Perhaps they're more cowardly. All I know is that I'd do it again. And I'm risking her to help you, and you have no idea how much is at stake now."

"Then why?"

"Because, Elodie, I can't let anything happen to you. If others found out what you know, they'd feel the same way. Like the director said, we need to be proactive. But as much as I love my daughter, I'm not hurting someone innocent to save her. What I've done to you already tears me up inside."

"Really?"

In ways he could never tell her. "Do you trust me?"

"You're really talking to her. Not just a clandestine chat here and there—you're part of her life. This isn't a way to lure me into compliance?"

He shoved his hands into his pockets and stared at the multicolored rug under his boots. "I thought I'd lost her. I was doing my duty, and against my best judgment, I didn't scour the earth for her after her wings were carved out. She had to endure her punishment. But there's so much more to the story, and she was—it was messed up. So when she was able to get word to me and needed my help? It was the least I could do for putting Numen before her."

Elodie's gaze softened, and she gazed at the ceiling. "My parents hear a lot working in the market. I get so frustrated with them. They know who's cheating on who. Which enforcer steals as much as he buys. Gossip on the senators. Oh, that's the good stuff. And I'd get so frustrated. I'd ask them, 'Don't you do more than listen?' and they'd forbid me from talking. Forbid it."

"Must've been frustrating."

She didn't nod, but her jaw was tight. "They told me to follow the rules. Don't question, and for a long time, I did. For a long time, I convinced myself that not making waves was for the best. I should want a quiet life like theirs. Then Tommy was killed, and I can't help but wonder if something my parents heard could've saved him."

"You can't know that."

She shook her head. "I can't. Making waves might've saved him, but my parents put the realm first. I think that's what's been missing. We've been putting the realm first. The humans first. Our leaders are forgetting to take care of our own people."

"I agree." And his decision was made. He crossed to the bed and began untying her ankle.

THE MORNING after the encounter with her mother, Persephone awoke, her lips still tingling from Urban's mouth on hers. The kiss had been straightforward, like he was.

How awkward would it be to train with him today?

In the bathroom, Kadee was securing her long hair in a bun. When she spotted Persephone in the mirror, she spun. "Did you really tell off your mother?"

"I... Yeah?" She was proud she'd stood up for herself, but a large part of her had just wanted to cry into her pillow last night. Instead, she'd fallen into an exhausted sleep before her fellow recruits had returned from training.

"I can't imagine. I heard your belongings are littering their lawn."

Persephone's heart sank. Her mother had actually gone through with it? All Persephone had was the barracks. She had no home. No friends. Only allies, which was more than she'd had before. "I guess I don't need them. I intend to be more useful than I was before."

"Your parents' lawn is probably pristine. I think it's just gossip. You know how that gets out of hand." Kadee snorted. "And yeah, you used to be a bit of a hag."

Persephone's relief was quick. For a girl who used to drive the gossip train, she was quick to buy into it. Hopefully, her mother hadn't emptied her room onto the grass. "A sea hag? Or like a swamp witch?"

Kadee returned to the mirror to finish her hair. "Like from the human stories? I didn't take you as having grown up on them—or that you identified with the princesses in the stories. You kind of are one, though."

"I was as nosy about the human realm as any other Numen. I haven't spent a lot of time there, and I'm not a princess."

The look she got said *Sure, you're not*. Seeing herself from a commoner's perspective was hard but long overdue.

"If Numen had princesses, I would've been one, but my parents would've rather traded me in," she admitted.

"I thought so." Kadee finished off her twist as if she hadn't just leveled Persephone's world.

"What?"

Kadee patted her head around the bun and gave her wings a small shake. "I like to watch people. Mac calls it creepy, but you learn a lot from watching, and people don't usually think I watch since I'm talking all the time. I like to talk—that's why being a watcher isn't a good fit for me. But a warrior? You get to watch people. And you and those friends of yours? You were all compensating. Since I grew up on human stories and we Numen are way closer to humans and their emotions than we like to admit, I could tell that you were all hurting in your own way and lashing out. After hearing about your run-in with your mom, I finished connecting the dots."

Persephone hugged her clothing to her chest. She needed to get changed quickly if she had a hope of grabbing something to eat before meeting Urban, but she wanted more of Kadee's refreshing insight. Someone had seen *her* through all of that. Someone real. Someone Persephone hadn't known existed, but the knowledge was just as critical.

She'd be lucky to count the female as a friend and an ally. "Nailed it."

Kadee beamed. "I gotta go. They got some berries to go with the paste they call oatmeal. Save you some?"

"Yes." She spun as she watched Kadee rush past her. "Please."

Kadee flashed a smile and was gone.

Persephone dressed and rushed downstairs to the lunchroom. She hadn't thought about failure before today. She'd been so set on trying, on rebelling, but for the first time, she thought she could do this. She could finish warrior training.

Floating on the new high from sitting at the table with the least popular warriors—Kadee, Mac, and Molly—she swept into the training room. Urban was standing in the middle, thumbing through his phone, a deep scowl etched onto his handsome face.

"Hey." She went for normal, or what she'd love to be their normal, if she didn't want kissing to be a bigger part of things. "Why did the coach go to the bank?"

Without looking up, he said, "He wanted his quarterback." He shoved the phone into his pocket. "Go ahead and stretch and run through the exercises we did yesterday. I've got to step out and call Ransom."

She was standing by the workout bench that doubled as her rest station when her back was fatigued. He wasn't even going to look at her as he left. "Urban?"

He paused at the door. "I know what you want to ask, and no, it can never happen again."

Hurt opened a deep cavern in her chest. "Never?"

He swept a hand around the room. "I'm in charge of your training. It wouldn't be right."

"We're both adults."

"Right. Then you understand."

She drew back. He was being unnecessarily curt. She thought of what Kadee'd said. Was he lashing out for other reasons, or was he ashamed of how he felt about her? "That I'm useless to the realm right now?"

His jaw tightened so hard she was surprised she didn't hear teeth crack; she'd used his words from that day in the market against him. "We talked about that. And this isn't the place for any more discussion. You'd better get started."

He left, and she was alone with tears pricking the backs of her eyelids. She swiped a hand across her dry cheeks. "Warriors don't cry."

She ran through the stretches, pushing her body past the limits she'd hit yesterday. Next were the exercises. And when Urban returned, his expression was back to being aloofly professional. His tone was impersonal, and he strode around the room like he had a whole group of broken angels to train.

But what bothered her the most was that he didn't share a joke. That was how she knew he'd shut her out. That she was nothing more to him than a job.

CHAPTER 6

Ransom slipped a hand around Elodie's elbow. They were standing in her small yard. It'd been two days since he'd called Sierra. His daughter had needed to talk to her mate, Boone, to decide what was best for Arik. He was the one they were all most concerned about.

Elodie peered at him. They'd been civil since she'd been untied. They took turns with the cooking, and he slept on the couch and had the crook in his neck to heal every morning to show for it. "You're really worried."

He nodded. "You'll see when we get there."

Her gaze softened; he liked seeing her less hostile and more trusting of him. Liked it a lot. Just like he enjoyed hearing her move around her bedroom when he was trying to fall asleep.

And then he'd wonder what it was like to have a home with someone like her. Go to bed with a person when he'd been alone for so long.

That way lay madness, and he had work to do.

Their wings were morphed, and Elodie was dressed in black linen pants and a plain blue shirt. Same canvas shoes, but this must've been how she'd normally dress if she were going to Earth for something other than luring demon-possessed humans into restroom stalls.

It was time to go. He closed his eyes and descended, noticing her strong grip on his elbow more than the change in environment. Crisp air surrounded him, and he knew what he'd see when he opened his eyes. Tall evergreens surrounding him. A dirt path that'd wind through the foothills to a breathtaking cabin with an even more gorgeous view. His daughter had found heaven on earth, and she'd made it a home.

But no home would be safe if she were perpetually in hiding.

"Welcome." Sierra stepped out of the shadows of two trees.

Ransom wanted to grin and hold his arms out for a big hug like he usually did, but he had to be conscious of Elodie's reaction. "Elodie. This is my daughter, Sierra."

Elodie crowded closer to him. She dipped her head but didn't make a move for a more formal greeting. Under their realm's current laws, she was risking her own wings by talking to Sierra. But she must've realized there were too many people who still associated with his daughter for their meeting to be a real threat.

Didn't mean there wouldn't be some punishment if the senate found out what they were doing. But that was why they were here.

Sierra cocked a brow. "Just want to rip the first bandage off?"

Elodie gazed at him. "There's more?"

So much more. He met her eyes. "Sierra's mother was ravaged by demons in the name of breeding. She's half demon."

Elodie's gasp scared birds out of nearby trees. She

yanked her hand off Ransom and took a step back. Her stunned gaze swiveled to Sierra. "You're a *demon?*"

"No," Sierra said, her tone brooking no argument. "I was born and raised in Numen as an angel and taught to serve our kind. Then I was blackmailed into turning on my team and I caved, lost my wings, and still managed to aid in keeping the realm safe. Would a demon do that?"

"B-but… It shouldn't be possible." Elodie backed up another step. "How?"

Ransom kept his voice gentle. "Our kind and theirs aren't that much different when you think about it. We're products of our environment and upbringing. Eons go by and you have angels—a peaceful kind serving humans and living in a pristine realm. From Earth we can gather all we need that we can't produce ourselves. And you have demons—a kind raised in a dark, noxious environment— that can procure no outside help. All they can do is attack humans to gain some sort of pleasure. They're our balance. Sierra's and Sandeen's sperm donors—for lack of a better description—were able to work through loopholes. Sierra's mom was a warrior and…" He had committed to telling Elodie everything, but they were risking everyone he was close to. Everyone, not just his daughter and grandson. He was struggling.

"Harlowe's my sister." Finishing the story, Sierra shrugged.

Elodie's eyes bugged open. "How many people know of you?"

"None but Papa until recently," Sierra answered. "Harlowe knows now. I've always known. Sandeen controls the metal mines in the underworld, whereas the senate used to broker females to his sire in order to get access to the metal."

"That's what got Tommy killed. He knew about Sandeen and the deal."

Sierra nodded. "Sandeen's mated to Harlowe. He can be a dick, but he's not evil."

Elodie folded her arms. "So, you two are in hiding but helping the realm, and you also think the senate is shady as hell?"

Ransom stepped in to answer this one. "Not everyone, but enough people are allowed to go unchecked, and it threatens Numen. Director Vale trusts only his team; he's using us to circumvent the various treasonous acts members of the senate are in on."

"It's Tommy's grandfather. He's the rot."

Ransom had always thought the elderly Senator Thomas was ambivalent, but he'd been a senator for literal centuries. It'd be long enough to give someone a god complex. He met Sierra's gaze, and she nodded. It was time for the last nugget of truth. The most precious part. "Then you understand why we haven't told the senate about Sierra. We're not just protecting her, but her human mate."

Elodie cocked her head. "We can't mate with humans."

Sierra's mouth quirked. "Just like we can't procreate with demons?" When Elodie pursed her lips, Sierra finished for him. "I have a son, and his father was a fallen."

There was no gasp. Just the wind rustling the needles on the trees. Elodie blinked. And blinked again.

"My grandson is important to me, Elodie," he said. "If you can't swear you'll keep him out of any vendetta and actively help us keep him safe, then we can't go any further." He didn't tell her they were in Montana. He wasn't sure how knowledgeable she was about nature on Earth, but perhaps she'd think they were on the fringes of the tundra.

"A kid? Fallen can have babies?" She propped her hands

on her hips. "I thought they were tossed into the elements to suffer."

Sierra fluttered her hands through her short hair. A bleak look passed over her face. "We suffer by being left in agony with no way to care for ourselves. If Boone hadn't found me, I don't know what would've happened. Pride and naivete gets most of us, but I'm not the only fallen with kids. The senate doesn't care about us—normally. They would be interested in a kid that's part fallen, part Numen, and part demon. I can never get back into Numen, and I don't care to find out if my son can, but someone up there might decide he's a threat—or worse, a thing to be studied or used."

Elodie's indignant inhale loosened the knot of tension in Ransom's chest.

"What do you think?" he asked. "You can turn back, and we won't hold you to anything, but you can help us come up with a plan. We'll keep you in the loop."

He'd have to assign someone to her. She could be a target if someone suspected she had the same information Tommy had.

She shook her head, her silky black hair flying. "No. No way. I'm in. Look." She held her hands up like she was proving she didn't have weapons. "I don't want kids hurt. And from what I've seen, if I can believe what you're all saying, then I'm in. I want to know it all, and I want to keep shit like trading females for metal from happening."

And that was what didn't sit right with him. Elodie wanted to be in the know. She felt like she'd been lied to her whole life, and she'd lost a friend because of it. She wanted retribution. She wanted a reaction. He wanted to keep his family safe. Were their individual goals destined to diverge?

~

AFTER AN EXCRUCIATING DAY of being close to Persephone, of smelling her sweet saffron-and-vanilla-bean scent, and watching her body flow through movement, growing smoother and stronger each day, he was shot. He wanted to shower, jack one off, and forget the way Persephone's hips flared in her sweatpants and how her breasts jutted out when she was stretching her hands over her head.

She was his trainee. He wasn't supposed to notice. He wasn't supposed to want to touch. He wasn't supposed to stop himself from telling her a joke every ten minutes.

She wasn't supposed to make him think of a future he'd sworn would never be for him. A future that included mates and bonds and no way to break free from someone stuck with you for eternity.

Persephone was trouble waiting to happen just for him. She'd be a problem if he hit on her while she was in training. Her parents were an issue. He hadn't spent a career getting hit on by senators or seeing the fallout of their treason to fall for the daughter of one.

He was a warrior.

He was also a warrior who was obsessed with a damaged angel who was stronger than he'd ever expected. An angel who'd been underestimated by everyone, including him. A female who was good at getting others to think what she wanted them to think. But convincing himself she was anything but genuine was a lost cause. She had her whole life in front of her, and she'd earned it. He wasn't going to stand in her way. And he wasn't going to throw himself across the busy highway that was a sync mate.

Nor was he going to drag her into the shit his team was getting into.

Ransom had contacted him, Bronx, Harlowe, Dionna, and Jagger. He and that female they'd hunted were planning to toss the blanket off the secrets of the realm, but for now, Ransom was doing it for Elodie, starting with Sierra. Urban was to stay in Numen and keep working with Persephone unless he was needed.

He was benched, and he wasn't even annoyed, which was what irritated him. He was getting too close to her. But she was progressing. He couldn't deny how far she'd come. She didn't wince as she stretched. She no longer needed breaks to sit, and she was practically bouncing off the walls.

At the same time, it sucked. She hadn't told him a joke since their kiss. He hated himself for the distance, but it was necessary.

His father's words drifted through his mind. *That wench I'm stuck with. You know what it's like having your soul attached to someone? To have no freedom? You want to become a warrior, you'd better be a damn good one, or you're going to find yourself stuck to a mate like your mother and be bonded together for fucking eternity.*

So what to do? He couldn't bring himself to release her to another trainer. She was growing close to Mac, Kadee, and Molly. She'd do fine. And wasn't that the issue? She'd do fine. She'd graduate and then she'd be in the field fighting real demons.

"Do another set," he barked. Persephone was working on knife moves but held not a blade in her hand but a weight. She'd be armed when she went to Stana, the female who'd take her through the rest of her training. Persephone was on track to join the same unit as her friends.

She flowed through the moves. Hell, she could probably do them in her sleep.

He came alert to a presence behind him. He spun to find Director Vale at the door. "Urban, a minute."

Urban dipped his head but spoke to Persephone. "If I'm not back before you're done, keep going through the exercises."

She would too. She was driven in a way he hadn't seen from her before. The Persephone in the workout room wasn't the Persephone who used to troll the realm with her minions. Neither was she the depressed Persephone from the nights he'd spent with her.

He stepped out, and the director beckoned him toward the stairs. They stood at the edge of the top step, alone in the hallway.

"What's going on?" Director Vale wasn't one for small talk, and Urban hated the sudden comprehension of the reason for his visit. "She's almost ready."

A dark brow ticked up. "She looks pretty bloody ready."

"She's not—" A hard look cut him off. He couldn't bullshit his boss, and it was time to admit his real issues. "Fine. She's ready, but I'm worried." The director waited for him to continue.

It took too damn long for Urban to come up with a valid reason for why he was worried. But there was one. His intuition wasn't gnawing only at his gut, afraid he'd become a lovesick fool. His mind spun. What was it? He'd been fighting his thoughts for a while, but once he delved into them, the answer was clear. "She's going to finish her realm training, and then she's going to go into the field. We can't replicate a demon attack up here, and the first vial of angel fire that gets brandished might make her freeze."

"She'll work with angel fire in her training."

"But it won't be a demon wielding it against her."

"None of us has that experience until it happens."

Exactly. "She's at a disadvantage."

The director did that gaze, the one where he looked through his subject like he was one of the humans' X-ray machines. "Is the worry about her…or you?"

"I'm protective; I won't deny it. I was there when she was hurt."

"Is that all?"

He could lie to his boss, but saying nothing was just as incriminating.

"Huh." Director Vale glanced down the hall, his expression contemplative. "Go to Earth. Take a few days, a week—I don't fucking care. But find some demons. Show her what she's getting into. See how she reacts around angel fire and whether she's willing to get over any hang-ups. Then—and this is critical—if she's still wanting to be a warrior, you get out of her fucking way."

Urban blew out a breath. Persephone would benefit from the exposure, but the director was doing this more for him. The time away would be nothing but a delay for Persephone's training. Yet he couldn't deny his willingness to snatch up the time. "Got it, boss."

The director nodded and took the stairs, lifting his wings high to keep from dragging them behind him.

Urban went back into the workout room. Persephone's light-brown skin glistened, her face a mask of concentration. She should be fatigued, but she wasn't letting her form get sloppy. "How's your back?"

He caught the near eye roll. "Good."

Yeah, he asked that a lot. It was a legitimate way to talk to her when he really wanted to ask her how she could tell which tree was a dogwood.

By the bark.

"The director wants to see how you'll do around demons before he clears you for training with a group."

She continued her flow, but her brow furrowed. "Do the other recruits do that?"

"The other recruits haven't had angel fire dumped on them."

Her jaw tightened but she didn't wince. "When do we go?"

"Now."

She straightened. "Don't I need to pack? Clean up?"

"Demons don't care about hygiene or whether you're rested."

"That's not what I was asking."

"No. We'll get what we need from the safe house that's set up for us." He'd arrange with Sierra where they'd go. Vegas was a typical spot, and the city would be a shock to the sheltered angel. That made it ideal.

CHAPTER 7

The trip to Earth didn't make sense, but it also made perfect sense. Persephone wasn't the typical trainee. She stared around her room in the two-bedroom condo Urban had taken her to in Las Vegas, then peeked out the window. The houses were almost all the same color, and she could feel the heat radiating off the glass.

She might not have gone to the human realm often, but she knew about the popular places. Angels loved to tell of their trips to the human world, and she'd listened like her life depended on it. Funny how it sort of did now. Her learning curve had been flattened. She'd heard so many tales of London, Paris, New York, Las Vegas, LA. And now she was in Vegas. Excitement rippled through her belly.

Her shoulders and back ached from the extra exercises she'd done for the day. The morph of wings, while painful during the transition, was more comfortable without their weight hanging off her back. When she'd told Kadee where she was going, the other girl had been shocked but understanding. Unlike the people Persephone had hung out with before, there was no jealousy oozing from Kadee, only support. Same with Mac and Molly when they'd come in while Persephone was grabbing her issued weapons. Going to Earth to hunt demons was unusual for a recruit, but none of them had been through what Persephone had.

She left the bedroom and found Urban on a stool at the island. The place was homier than her parents' mansion and she greatly preferred it. Warriors often spent more time on Earth, and Persephone was suddenly looking forward to those days. "Okay. What next?"

Urban scrolled on his phone. "We go to the Strip and walk around."

"Just…walk around?"

He nodded. "The car's in the garage."

She hadn't seen the garage when they'd descended to a closed-off veranda by the sliding back door. Urban had muttered something about safe houses being easier to set up in warmer climates. Patios and sun blocks. Made transcending directly into a hidden place possible.

He finally glanced up. "How's the back?"

A lot better if he'd quit asking. For the last two weeks, it was all about her back. Her back could take so much more than a month ago. Each time she made it through a flare of pain, she set the bar higher. Her tolerance and strength were growing, and she'd caught herself moving with no pain, no restriction. Only the mornings sucked, as after she'd healed all night, her muscles and skin had tightened up.

"How about we strike a deal?" she asked. "I'll tell you if my back is bothering me. You don't need to ask anymore."

"Fine." His gaze flicked down her body. "Is that what you're wearing?"

He didn't sound impressed. They were supposed to be hunting demons, but since she hadn't trained with weapons—only the movements that went with them—she hadn't worn her full outfit. She'd stand out. But she didn't wear sandals and a gown like she would going out in Numen. Instead, she'd chosen a pair of skinny jeans from the variety of styles and sizes in the bedroom and a tight-fitting blouse. This wasn't her first time in human clothing, but the pants took some getting used to. On her feet were leather boots with a minimal heel. Whoever stocked the place knew how to blend while also being functional.

She looked down at herself. "Should I change?"

"No. It's a good choice."

He rose, and she bit her cheek. Wow. He wore the same long-sleeved black shirt, but from what she understood, even long sleeves in a Vegas summer wouldn't draw attention. The jeans, though. The black pants he usually wore showed his frame, but the dark material had hidden more than she thought. His thighs in blue jeans looked more rounded, more powerful, and when he twisted to grab a set of keys from a dish on the island, the shirt cinched at his waist, and his ass was *fire*.

When he turned back, he caught her looking before she lifted her eyes from his butt. Heat filled her cheeks. "Ready?" she squeaked.

His brows drew together. "No."

"Okay?"

"What do they call the Terminator when he retires?"

Taken aback, she stared. Why was he telling a joke? They hadn't shared one for weeks. "The Exterminator."

His lips twitched, and a beat of satisfaction passed through his eyes. "All right. Now we're ready."

"Was that a test?"

"I'm reminding you who you are," he said over his shoulder as he crossed through the kitchen and exited through a door in a little nook around the corner.

Her frustration growing, she followed him out. She'd been shut out for so many days, she'd given up hope there could be more to their relationship. Then he'd busted out a joke. "Excuse me?"

"Get in."

She glanced at the red sedan. "No."

"Do as you're told, or I won't clear you for training."

This wasn't the male who'd lain in her bed telling her jokes and being a general comfort to her. "Maybe you forgot who you are."

He prowled back around the car. "I'm your trainer."

She didn't move from her position by the door. "Then who was the guy beside me in bed? Where's he?"

"He's not sending a damaged female he cares about into battle."

Damaged was a slap to the face, while the confession of his care was a soothing touch. "You're confusing me."

"You're confused? I'm going out of my damn mind, Persephone. I agree with your parents."

"How dare you!"

"I dare because I care," he said hotly, stalking toward her until he loomed over her.

She couldn't stop the giggle. The rhyme was absurd in the middle of their argument. "You're a poet and didn't know it."

His expression only grew more pained. "Percy." He dipped his head, and his lips landed on hers.

She groaned. Finally. The stoic male trainer was once again the guy who used to sneak through her window. She fisted her hands in his shirt. They were supposed to hunt demons, but she didn't want to move. She didn't want this to stop.

He must have been thinking the same because he pushed her against the door. Her breath whooshed out of her. The sting from the pressure against her back wasn't bad, but being overpowered by him was intoxicating.

Pulling away, concern flashed in his eyes. "Shit—sorry."

Her injuries were not ruining this. She tugged his head down until his mouth was back on hers. This time he groaned and sank his hands into the flesh of her ass.

"Do you know how amazing you look in these pants?" he growled against her lips.

"No… Tell me."

He kissed his way down her neck as he massaged her butt cheeks. His grip was firm, unyielding, and for once, he wasn't concentrating on her scars. Right then, she was a desirable female to him.

She stuffed her hands through his silky hair. He tugged her shirt from her waistband.

Logic was struggling to return. What if he were stalling? What if this was a ploy to keep her from going into the field? But her top was rolled past her breasts and his warm hands cupped her sides.

What if she could have both?

She wasn't strong enough to turn him down, but she'd take it only so far, then grab the keys from him and threaten to drive if he didn't take her to the Strip.

THIS WAS AN EVEN BIGGER mistake to add to the kiss in the workout room, but Urban had been toast once he caught sight of Persephone in human clothing. The garments showed way more of her curves than even the thin robes she used to wear in Numen.

He couldn't see anything beyond sleek thighs that would anchor perfectly around his hips. A dip on each side of her waist like they were made for his hands to hold her to him.

And now that his flesh was touching hers, entirely too many clothes were in the way. Was it crude to undress her in the garage? He was a dying man, and seeing her naked was the only remedy. Tasting her was the only antidote.

The swells of her breasts were mesmerizing, and they were right there. He caught a cloth-covered nipple in his mouth and worked her bra cup down on the other side. Her hands roamed through his hair, and each breath she inhaled brought her chest closer. Each exhale, farther away, like a taunt.

When his finger landed on a bare nipple, he nearly came in his jeans. Not only was he in the longest dry spell of his adult life, but he couldn't recall such anticipation for being with a female. She drove him wild.

He moved his mouth to the second tight peak and licked around the hot flesh as he worked the rest of her bra from her body. She squirmed against him, a moan leaving her lips.

If she was this responsive to him just touching her tits, how would she be when his hands were on other areas?

He was dying to know.

Undoing her jeans, he kept up his mouth play on her nipples, loving the way her fingers twined in his hair when she really liked what he was doing. Sliding a hand between her underwear and skin, he worried about how long he'd last. His restraint was dwindling the more he got to see and feel.

The material of her jeans had enough give that he didn't need to fully undress her. When his fingertips hit her wet heat, she bucked against him.

"Like that?" He almost smiled against the fevered flesh of her breasts. He wasn't asking how her back was.

"Yes," she groaned, her hips rolling into his touch.

He slid through her wet seam and back and circled her clit.

"It's not going to take long, Urban," she said between panted breaths.

He hadn't been with anyone for so long, and they were doing this in a dark garage. She was a silk-sheets-and-soft-mattress kind of female. She was raised in luxury. Clarity struck, dousing him with a bucket of water, but then his name left her lips.

"Urban…keep going."

So he did. The excruciating pinch of his zipper was his penance for crossing a line he shouldn't. But it was worth it. She rocked her hips, and he wedged his hand in far enough to keep pressure on her clit while sliding a finger inside her. He continued switching his attention between her taut nipples until she went rigid under him and heat flooded his hand.

"Urban!" She clenched her fists into his shirt, arched, and slammed into the door. "Ow, dammit."

That was the rest of the ice bath he needed. He'd fucked up. He yanked his hand out of her pants and straightened. "Shit. How's your—"

She plastered a finger over his lips. "If you ask how my back is one more time, you're not getting my mouth on your cock."

He jerked, shock hitting him across the head like a baseball bat, but it was nothing in the face of the lust crowding every cell of his body. "You shouldn't—"

"We went past 'shouldn't' way before you gave me an excellent orgasm." Her hands were working at his fly; he was too stunned to stop her.

"Persephone." When she paused and met his gaze, a dark brow arched like she was asking why he was interrupting her efforts to access his erection, he almost lost the words he meant to say. "This is wrong."

"You wanted to delay demon hunting, and I'm okay with it—for now." The sound of his zipper opening resonated through the garage.

He struggled to stay coherent, but this was too important. Clasping his hand over hers, he waited until she stilled. "I wasn't doing this to put off getting you in the field." The uncertainty in her eyes gutted him. Didn't she think he'd want her otherwise? "This?" He dropped his gaze to where her shirt had fallen to half cover her tits, then up to her wide brown eyes. "Is us. It's not the job. It's not anything else. It's me being unable to resist you, which has been a growing problem."

She searched his face like she was looking for a hint he was lying, then a smile curved her lush lips. Stroking the front of his pants, she purred, "This seems to be growing."

"It's been a problem."

"Then let me take care of it." She slid down his body to kneel, and he froze.

"You don't have to."

Gazing up at him, her expression was guileless, a look he paired with the real Persephone. "Do you want me to?"

He blew out a gusty breath. "Fuck yeah."

She flipped open the button, the last restriction holding back his erection, and took him out in her warm hand. When her lips wrapped around the tip, he was ready to blow.

Don't do it. If he looked, he'd come right away, but he wanted to enjoy what she was doing. Something he never thought would or should happen. He tipped his head back. It was his turn to sink his hands into her hair. Impossibly softer and silkier than he'd imagined, and he'd fantasized a lot.

"Percy."

She hummed against him, and his ball sac tightened until it was nearly painful. Rocking his hips, he kept his movements short. Ramming his dick into the back of her mouth wasn't going to make this enjoyable for her.

But she sucked him in farther, and he was done. Just done. "Perse—"

Like she knew he was warning her, she grabbed on to his ass and ran her tongue along his length.

Fire laced down his spine and straight out of his cock. A long, deep groan emanated from his chest, a guttural sound he'd never made before, and he released into the hot depths of her throat. Through the blinding ecstasy, he managed to keep his grip loose on her hair, but he had to release her or wrench her head in the wrong direction with the force of his orgasm. Planting a hand against the door, he rode wave after wave of his climax until he sagged and she finally released him. He had to squeeze his eyes shut for a moment, not caring that his deflating dick was hanging out.

That was intense.

When he opened his eyes, she was wiping off her mouth and straightening her clothing. "Ready?"

No. He should've learned by now, he'd never be ready for this female.

CHAPTER 8

$\mathcal{R}$ansom walked with Elodie down a trail that led to a sparkling lake. Arik was napping, and Sierra and Boone wanted to get some work in while they could. Ransom had used the time to introduce Elodie to another part of the truth, one she'd already known but could be just as astonishing as meeting his daughter and grandson. That part of the truth would arrive soon.

Elodie had been quiet since they'd arrived. She'd held back from Arik when he was in the same room, hovering at the edges until the boy toddled toward her and fell on his bum at her feet.

Ransom couldn't deny that watching her unlocked something inside himself. He loved being a dad, but he'd missed raising Sierra with someone who really cared. Sharing looks whenever Sierra cut a new tooth or took flight for the first time. It'd been just him. But when Arik had plopped onto the floor and smiled up at Elodie, she'd looked to Ransom. Her eyes misted, and her lips curved up. And that was when he knew. She understood how critical it was to keep the baby safe. To protect his daughter, who'd once been an innocent like his grandson. Who'd been forced into making a terrible mistake and had paid dearly for it. Like his mother, Arik would likely grow to serve the realm.

"He doesn't have wings?" She stopped, her shoes scratching at the dirt.

"You've been dying to ask that for two weeks."

"It felt rude."

Instead, they'd spent their days in nearby towns gathering supplies for her—new clothing and shoes. He showed her Sierra and Boone's shop that'd become Sierra's headquarters, where she still did IT work for the team, and between excursions, he'd recounted as much as he could about what he knew of the treasonous plots his team had dealt with.

"It's pertinent. No, he doesn't have wings. We don't know if he's immortal." His throat thickened as he spoke. Arik was a first for their kind. "His father was a fallen and his mother fell when she was pregnant. So…that's all we can assume. Children of fallen don't get wings."

Her brows drew together. "What are the odds the senate knows that?"

He hadn't thought of it, but he should've. The answer was obvious. "Pretty good. They've meddled with the records of fallen before."

She started walking again. "This Sandeen—does he have young?"

"No, but he's not fallen, and we think he got into the realm because his intentions were, for lack of a better word, angelic." That wasn't how he'd describe Sandeen, but the male had proven himself.

A deep male voice spoke from ahead. "How dare you toss around accusations." Sandeen emerged from the trees.

Ransom hadn't suspected he was close by. The guy was good.

Harlowe stepped out behind him, rolling her eyes. Then her steady gaze settled on Elodie.

Elodie's eyes were wide, then narrowed. "You look like us."

"My horns and fangs were burned off."

She blanched, her gaze straying to Harlowe's regretful expression.

Sandeen winked at his mate. "She misses the horns."

Harlowe clicked her tongue. "You're shameless. Anyway, this is the other half demon we know about."

Sandeen's face grew grim. "I'm afraid there might be another."

"What?" Ransom and Elodie said in unison.

He nodded. "On my way to the mines yesterday, I found signs of one of your robes in the Gloom. It was bloody."

Just like the Mist was the in-between of Numen and Earth, the Gloom separated Earth and Daemon. "A female?"

Sandeen shrugged. "I don't know, but I'm going to hunt them down."

Elodie swung her head around to look at them all. "You know what that means, right? They're still trafficking females to create more halflings."

Harlowe's nod was grim. "It's something we'll have to rule out."

"It could be from before," Sandeen said. "A victim who's been kept all this time like my mother was."

Elodie's eyes widened. The note of sorrow for a female he'd never known was clear in Sandeen's voice, and she had picked up on it.

"What can we do?" Ransom asked.

"Train her," Harlowe replied, tipping her head toward

Elodie. "As long as she doesn't fuck up and contact someone in Numen, she's safe here. But someone reported her to the director because they wanted her to quit digging. They might've wanted to test us and how far we're willing to go to keep the secret. But she needs to learn to defend herself."

"I can," Elodie said. At their dubious looks, her lower lip puffed out. "I had some training from my parents before I started coming to Earth."

"How were you able to leave the realm?" Ransom asked. Angels needed permission. Senators' kids usually didn't need a reason. Their excuses were often flimsier than wet cardboard, but Elodie had been born to what would be considered the middle class in Numen. The working class who kept the realm running.

"More and more earthly possessions are in demand. Father needed help, so I worked for him as a courier. Tommy would help me when he was bored, and that was when he started checking into all the stories he'd heard."

Made sense. "I can help train her. She needs weapons."

"Oh, I've got weapons." Sandeen grinned, a smile that would've either terrified Elodie or made her start unbuttoning her shirt. The male had that effect on females, and he didn't have to try. But Harlowe was the only being to hold his interest.

Elodie drifted closer to Ransom, and if that didn't start a warm, protective glow in his chest.

Still, Ransom wanted to wipe the grin off the male's face in case Elodie was a little entranced. He cleared his throat. "Okay. We'll work on hand to hand until you get back."

His pulse picked up. Why was he looking forward to touching Elodie again? Where had his professionalism gone? As the father of a warrior, he didn't like the thought that someone so close to Sierra could be lusting after her. It was uncalled-for and could affect safety in the field.

Unfortunately, theirs was an usual situation, and Elodie was a beautiful female. He was inexperienced in working around an innocent who wasn't tied to his team or a human target. That was all. He hoped the anticipation running through his veins would get the memo.

"Two o'clock," Persephone said. People milled around them in the casino. Urban was sitting near the food court with her. It was after nine at night, and he had begun the training session by having Persephone identify and classify possessed hosts and free demons.

"My two or yours?" Urban asked. They were on a bench, facing each other like other young couples who couldn't get enough of each other.

He hadn't gotten enough of her.

"Crap." She frowned. "My two would be your ten?" He dipped his head. "Your ten, then."

He nodded. He'd spotted the human she referenced five minutes ago. "Type?"

"Ew, archmaster. They really are ugly, aren't they?"

"Not one for bent yellow fangs and pus dripping from facial boils?"

"Gross."

He chuckled. Never had he had fun demon spotting. It wasn't a sport. In the old days, he'd be with his team. They'd pretend to be tourists, talking into their phones or furiously messaging, while they planned to take on the archmaster possessing the human. But this time he'd have to report the possession to another team. He was alone with Persephone, and while she needed experience, it wasn't wise to take on an archmaster with only a trainee. Just because he could do it didn't mean he should.

"I'll send the info in." He managed to get a photo and sent the details to the director. His boss would pass the intel down to another team, keeping Urban and Persephone's presence out of it.

"Oh, wow," she breathed, her eyes widening in the direction over his shoulder.

He didn't know what she saw, but she was making a critical error. "No staring."

Her gaze jerked to his. "Do sylphs really run in packs like that?"

"They aren't organized, but there's usually more than one."

"They're like the rats of the underworld."

"Yep." He added that to his message to the director.

"Aren't we going to deal with them? I can take a sylph."

She hadn't taken anything, not even in training. "No. For one, there are four of them. I can't get us all into the Mist—that'd be a challenge for both of us. And if I thought we could both do it, then where could we do it and not be seen vanishing?"

She glanced around. People stood in front of each restaurant in the food court. People were pouring out of a show that had just finished. "The bathroom?"

"Both of us? Some people might sound the alarm if the two of us walked into a bathroom together. They're not unisex."

Her mouth pursed. "There's a lot of strategy."

"Patience and strategy are the most important parts of being a warrior. Situational awareness is paramount, or we risk humans, we risk discovery, and we risk our wings." Her wings were too beautiful to be severed from her body.

Her morph was becoming one of the most irritating

things about roaming the human realm with her. He wanted to know what she looked like, head thrown back, wings arched behind her as her breasts jutted out and he thrust—

He shifted to sit with his back against the wall, hoping the movement redirected blood flow away from his dick. "If we find a symaster, then we'll hunt."

"Like that guy?"

A red-faced, middle-aged man limped through the wide corridor. His expression turned more disgruntled when he saw the number of people ordering food. Symasters couldn't fully possess a human, but all demons' goals were to disrupt a human so an archmaster could take possession of their soul, and this symaster was making his human ride nice and irritated. The man was on his way to hating life and wishing away anything for a break from the constant bad luck plaguing him.

While Urban watched the man out of the corner of his eye, Persephone pretended to study her nails as she bobbed her leg over one knee. The sylphs scattered in front of the human. Whatever old knee injury he'd experienced had flared, likely due to the symaster's influence. The creatures weren't corporeal, but they could influence enough energy to make a person clumsy or cause bad shit to happen. The sylphs tripped the man. He stumbled, shouted a swear word, and leaned over, gripping his knees, his sides heaving.

"That poor man."

"He'll have some relief tonight after we're done with that demon."

The satisfied smile she gave him warmed his heart. She'd delight in taking out the symaster after seeing how he affected the already struggling human.

She dropped her voice to a whisper. "He's heading toward the exit."

"Perfect. He's probably going to the parking ramp." Those structures were ideal hunting grounds for warriors. Naturally shadowed, and the cameras were often grainy and had blind spots. It was easier to explain a blip of two people disappearing when there were no human witnesses to back it up. And Sierra could tap into the network and delete the footage when necessary.

They got up and walked behind the human. Urban slung his arm around Persephone's slim shoulders. She leaned into him, and if the pressure on her back hurt, she didn't mention it. Her giggle was fake, but only because he knew her. He'd heard that same laugh throughout the market; after hearing her real laughter, he could easily perceive the clear division between when she was genuine and when she wasn't.

He liked the real giggles better.

She put her hand on his chest and chuckled again. "That was fun. I can't wait to get you back to the room."

If the human could hear them, he'd think they were a horny couple on their way to a fuckfest.

Didn't he wish.

Urban lowered his head to murmur in her ear. "When he gets to his car, I'll take the lead. You follow, and when we get to the Mist, stay back. Give us room to fight, and always watch your back."

Wide eyes looked up at him. "There's demons in the Mist?"

"Shouldn't be, but you never know." The realm was too ambiguous. It took training and a good sense of location to cross back and forth. "Sometimes one gets away from a fight and isn't immediately expelled." He clenched his jaw. "Sometimes, a warrior loses a fight."

She stiffened but nodded.

He wasn't trying to scare her on purpose. This whole trip could be proof that he was attempting to drive her away from being a warrior, but the longer she was on Earth, the more they'd watched and she hadn't panicked. She'd soaked up knowledge, and she wasn't overly giddy for a fight, but she also wasn't champing at the bit to get her hands bloody. He could concede she was warrior material.

They went down the stairs while the human took the ramp. Behind him, they strolled while the man limped down the breezeway. If he had to take the elevator, they'd watch the numbers and race up or down the stairs. The man wasn't moving fast enough to ditch them.

The breezeway went to the main level, but the human got into the elevator. Urban slowed their pace. The whirring cables running the elevator got louder the closer they got.

"Three," Persephone said.

They rushed the stairwell and raced up three floors. When they emerged, the muttering of the human could be heard, making him easy to find. Even better, no one else was within view. Urban shoved his hands into his pockets, looking nonchalant but intent on getting to his ride, and let his long strides eat up the space between him and the human.

Persephone's quicker footsteps pattered behind him. He couldn't worry about her now. As long as she was safe, all she needed to do was spectate.

Urban got close just as the man was fumbling with his keys. He stayed behind their target, hoping Persephone knew that the human shouldn't witness them disappearing either. The man would be disoriented but not clueless.

Slamming a hand through the demon, he muttered the words that'd take them into the Mist.

Cool droplets surrounded him. Persephone's gasp told him she was there.

The demon snarled and spun, lashing out with its claws. Urban danced back and kicked the thing in the face. He slid a knife from the holster under his shirt just as the demon jumped up, and slammed the blade into the creature's bony rib cage.

The symaster roared, revealing dripping fangs, and Urban kicked him again. This underworld type was more animalistic than an archmaster. It fell, and Urban dove in, yanked his knife out and stuffed the blade into the demon again. The cry this time was strangled. He stomped his boot on the thing's neck and kept it immobile.

He yanked his vial of angel fire from around his neck and held it out to Persephone. "Here."

She paled, her gaze stuck on the crystal vial of plasmatic fluid.

"Percy. Do it." This was exactly the test she needed, and she was failing.

"I-it's down, though."

"There's no need for honor fighting demons. They'll kill you with your pants down." The demon was struggling, its sharp claws gouging his boots. Urban was willing to sustain a few injuries, but he couldn't be brash.

She held her hands to her chest like she was afraid Urban would grab them and make her physically hold the vial.

"Persephone." He winced as the demon's claws raked through his boot leather and tore through his pants. The creature was going to panic and become more destructive, and while Urban would heal, he couldn't regrow limbs.

"I..." Her face ashen, she took a step back.

"Shit." Urban uncapped the vial, dumped the contents on the demon, and stepped out of the way. It screeched once the burning started. A strangled sound made him look for Persephone, but she was no longer there. "Ah, hell."

He put the cap back and tucked the vial into his pocket. Duty dictated he stayed until the demon was dead.

When there was nothing left, he stuffed a hand through his hair. Had he pushed her too far? Or had he pushed her far enough?

Exposing her to angel fire had had to be done, but he couldn't stop feeling like an ass. After some training, she might've been bolder. The trauma response might've been diluted by confidence. Or her reaction was inevitable, and she wasn't cut out to be a warrior.

He didn't have the answers, but he'd have to find her.

She'd failed. Urban had tested her, and she'd failed.

Seeing so many demon-affected humans was awful. The demon itself was a creature that nightmares were tailored after. But the small bottle of angel fire petrified her. She couldn't touch it, nor could she have had the courage to dump it on a living thing.

Urban had been around her the entire time with that vial around his neck, but it was a part of him she hadn't questioned. He was a warrior. The vial was something they never left home without. She'd be expected to have one on a chain or in a pocket. And if she used it, causing the same excruciating pain she knew intimately, she risked getting a drop or more on herself.

Her hands shook as she rubbed them together. She was crouched right inside the door of the safe house. She'd crossed directly from the Mist to the safe house—a dangerous game of chance since she wasn't properly trained in navigating the nebulous in-between realm. But she'd wanted to leave so badly, and home was the last place she wanted to go, where her parents would tell her how right they were. She knew of nowhere else to go, and her last happy memory was of being in the garage with Urban. Kissing him. She'd envisioned the private cove built around the sliding door. One step and she'd crossed from the Mist to the human realm.

The door whisked open, and Urban walked through. All the lights were off, and shadows surrounded them. Ambient light from the street outside filtered around the cracks in the blinds in the front room. His boots were the only thing within view, but a metallic stench touched her nose.

"Are you bleeding?" Had her hesitation cost him?

"I'll heal."

She bit her cheek. "I'm sorry. You got hurt because of me."

He crouched, resting his arms across his knees. "That was the point of tonight. To see what you're ready for."

"I failed."

"With angel fire, yes."

She couldn't bring herself to look at his face. Instead, she stared at his boots, the rips in his pants. One of his legs had been shredded from his ankle to right below his knee. His position had to be painful. "I'm sorry."

"Are you going to quit?"

She squeezed her eyes shut. His question was without emotion. She couldn't tell whether he was disgusted with her or... What else was there? She was disappointed in herself.

Was she going to quit? And do what? Being a senator

was never something she'd sought to do. Politics were nothing but the magnified version of the silly games she played, roaming the realm and flaunting her status. She'd like to think she was smart enough to be an analyst, but she wanted to actively help others. She didn't want to help them die like a chaperone or record their daily grind like a watcher.

She'd worked with Urban, and she'd been doing well. Until now.

"How about this?" he asked. "Do you *want* to quit?"

She worked her lower lip through her teeth. The answer came to her instantly, but she was afraid to say it.

"Persephone."

"No. I don't want to. But maybe I should."

"Why?" When she looked up, he shrugged. "We can work with you as long as you don't want to quit. I'll get a replacement vial, and we'll go back out."

She continued chewing her lip. Good thing she could heal or she'd have a bloody lip tomorrow. "Just like that?"

"Yes. Wait here." He rose and went for the stairs. Their bedrooms were up there, and of course he'd have more supplies.

"We're going back out now?" Panic hammered at her brain in rhythm with her heart.

"Dunno."

Irritated at herself for the way she'd reacted and how she was acting now, she pushed off the floor, flipped the light on, and slid onto a stool at the island. She propped her elbows on the counter and visually traced the faux marble veins.

When Urban returned, he sat next to her. A *tink* on the counter drew her gaze to the noise. She flinched. A vial of angel fire was attached to a delicate chain that had no business holding something so deadly. She slumped. An inanimate object and she was overreacting. It wasn't like the object could dump itself on her.

"That one's for you to wear."

Her heart rate shot up. "What?"

"Trainees get issued one early on. They have to get comfortable with it, almost to the point of forgetting they even have it. Yet also stay so damn aware of the danger they carry right over their heart. It's going to be second nature to reach for it and dump it on a demon." He pushed it closer to her with the tip of his pinkie. "But first, you have to put it on."

The ache in her back brought all the memories back. The burning. The terror. The humiliation. The months of healing afterward. More shame. She let her gaze wander over the facets of the crystal container. It was small. Not even an ounce, but it didn't take much of the substance to decimate its target.

She mimicked Urban's movement and touched the tip of her pinkie to the cool vial. She didn't push it closer to him, just maintained contact. She and the angel fire had a stare-off.

She needed to put it on.

"Why am I so scared?" she whispered.

"Because it changed your life."

It had. She'd suffered. But she'd come through. The throbbing between her wings was more mental than physical at this point.

Angel fire had changed her life, but it didn't ruin it. She'd been used. Duped. But she refused to take responsibility for terrible people. The angel fire had severed the binds she'd encased herself with after a lifetime of being told who to be.

Angel fire had set her free. And she'd gladly wear the scars to show it.

Curling her hand around the vial, she barely registered her quickened breathing. One smooth move, and the chain was over her head, the vial resting against her sternum. For once, Urban's stony gaze shifted to surprise. He kept his under his shirt. She'd do the same.

She dropped the vial between her skin and her top and swallowed hard. "This is a tool. And I could get hurt from it again, but I'll come back stronger than before. Just like last time."

An eyebrow ticked up, but the pride in his dark eyes was priceless. When had someone ever looked at her like that? "Ready to go back out?"

"Absolutely."

CHAPTER 9

Ransom gauged Elodie's movements. In the last few days, she'd gotten better at not transmitting her intentions in her expressions. Right now, her eyes were darting down to his groin. She was planning to kick him in the nuts to get out of the corner he'd boxed her in while they trained in the shop-turned-gym on Sierra's property.

"Not going to work," he said, hands up and gauging her face while he waited to attack.

Elodie's expression hardened, and she darted one way first, then the other. She almost snuck past him, but she spun and decided to kick him in the privates after all.

An *oomph* left him. He dropped to his knees and toppled onto the mat. Her small foot made it easier to dig in and decimate his balls. "Fuck."

She lowered herself to her knees next to him. "Oh, no. I thought you said I need to try to hit you there if there's no other way. Did I really hurt you?"

He gave her an incredulous look and struggled to catch his breath when what he really wanted to do was vomit.

Angels' healing power did not prevent them from experiencing pain.

"Your face is red." Her tone was accusatory, but the line across her brow and the way she hovered projected her concern.

"No, no," he gasped. "It's effective." He hadn't been prepared for her to get one over on him. Kudos to Elodie. Shame on him for underestimating his opponent. He deserved a crushed-nut reminder.

But it hurt.

He dropped one hand onto the mat and cupped his precious balls with the other. Rocking back and forth, he rode through the pain. Elodie hung next to him, moving with him and inspecting his face.

"Seriously." His voice was stronger now. "It's okay. You did exactly what you're supposed to."

She sat on her ass since it was clear he wouldn't be going anywhere soon. "What do you do if a demon nails you there?"

"Howl like a creature from Daemon and fight through the pain." But demons were more concerned with impaling, ripping, and tearing. They'd rather mutilate than jab and run.

"I won't do it again." Her ponytail hung over her shoulder, and her lips were set in a pouty line.

He gutted through shifting to sit next to her, then clasped her hands. "No, you did exactly what you were supposed to, and you taught me I have to stay sharp, no matter the opponent." A shadow lingered over his thoughts. "Sometimes I feel like I need more reminders than I should."

"Why?"

Maybe it was because his guts still felt like they were going to evacuate his body through his penis, but he answered. "I was out of the field for so long, and then when I got sent back, it was to work with rookies. I've been sidelined more than I've been in action, and it shows."

"You took a step back to be around for Sierra?"

Nostalgia coursed through him, prompting a smile. "I stepped back to be a dad. You know how warriors get paired with a mate when their situation is dire?" She nodded. "I never did. Year after year went by, and I stayed alone. I thought for sure I'd get the sync mark, but…nothing."

Surprising him, she nodded matter-of-factly. "I know what you mean. I thought Tommy was my path to a long life with someone I liked enough to spend eternity with."

"Shouldn't you more than like your eternal mate?" He was mostly joking, but her gaze was torn when she met his.

"I didn't love him." Tears glittered in her eyes.

"Hey." He scooted closer. "It's okay."

"No, it feels wrong to admit. He was head over heels for me, and I liked him—I cared deeply about him—but I wasn't in love." She blew out a hard breath. "This is the first time I've admitted it."

She'd probably tried to convince herself she'd been in love with him after he was killed. "May I ask—"

"Why I'm so young and was willing to settle down for centuries with a close friend?" She picked at her nails. She was wearing black athletic shorts and a baggy shirt like him, but he still noticed her bare skin way too much. "I wanted what my parents have. I still do, I guess."

"I get that. My parents had me really late in their marriage, and by the time I was an adult, they were done with life. They walked into the fire." Angel fire was a weapon, but it was also an out for Numen who tired of their existence. The large fountain of angel fire in the middle of Numen was their supply and their exit plan.

She scooted to face him and cupped his hand in hers. "I'm sorry."

He lifted a shoulder. "A couple like them wasn't nearly as heartbreaking as many who walk into the fire. They were happy. Content. I miss them.

"I trust my team with my life. They have my back. But I still go to bed alone. I return to Numen, to an empty house."

She tilted her head up, her eyes warm. "You're a really good guy, Ransom."

"Even if I keep a few secrets?"

She looked around them. "I understand why some secrets need to be kept, but too many people are paying the price."

"I agree." They'd had this talk several times, like Elodie was trying to work through her justifications for why she needed to blow the lid on everything that had been happening.

"How's your…" Her gaze dropped to his crotch, and a blush stained her cheeks.

If he were any of the many males he'd trained over the years, he'd have made some lewd comment about having her check, but he'd never do such a thing. Only now he was thinking it, and blood flowed to his aching dick. "Fine," he said hoarsely. "They'll be fine."

"If you were a human, you wouldn't be walking right for a few days. I got you good."

"Good thing I don't use it very often." He chuckled before he realized the confession that had just left his mouth. He was way too comfortable around Elodie.

Her eyes widened. "You don't?"

"Sorry, I didn't mean to get personal, but I guess I'm not ashamed of not sleeping around." A lot of his kind had adopted a life of promiscuity since the thought of settling for eternity with one other person could be daunting. That was fine, of course, but he'd never bought into that attitude. "I like sex, but when Sierra was little, it was impossible. And when she was older, well, it wasn't like I could get close to someone, so it was either a string of one-night stands or constantly breaking up with someone. I chose solitude."

"Tommy and I didn't…" She grimaced. "I can't believe I'm telling you this."

He chuckled. "Likewise, but I don't mind." He wanted to know everything about her sex life.

She went back to picking at her fingers. "I didn't initiate, and I think he thought we were waiting until we were mated." She held her hands up as if perplexed. "You're easy to talk to. With your looks, I'm surprised someone hasn't latched on to you."

"My looks?" Females didn't talk to him this way. Or did they and he didn't care to notice? He noticed Elodie.

She rolled her eyes, but the blush deepened. "You know, those curls?" She reached up and ruffled the hair on top of his head. It brought her closer, and the wildflowers-in-rain scent of her surrounded him. "They're adorable, and those baby-blue eyes, and with the angles of your face, you're very attractive." She met his gaze, and her lips parted. She snatched her hand back and resettled on her butt.

"Thank you," he said softly. "I'm not sure which I like more—that I'm easy for you to talk to or that you find me attractive."

Shy, she looked away. "It really shouldn't be either one. I mean, if I don't play by your rules, I might endanger your daughter and that cherub of a grandson. Then what?"

"Will you endanger them?" Was she trying to scare him away?

"No," she whispered. "Sierra and Sandeen were innocent once."

"Sandeen would deny that."

She smiled. "He's not what I expected. Sierra either. It shows just how much we need to find that female."

If there was one. But there'd be more if the senate was allowed to keep their secrets. "If she's out there, we'll find her. And we'll make those responsible pay."

Elodie's gaze was earnest, and she grabbed his hand again. "That's all I want."

He squeezed her fingers, but they didn't break apart. She rose up on her knees again and pressed a soft kiss to his lips. His balls proved they hadn't fully healed, but he'd gladly weather the ache if it got her opening up to him again.

"Now." Urban was struggling with the symaster. Persephone jumped forward, mentally reciting the mantras Urban had made her say, and dumped the vial of angel fire on the creature's back. It shrieked, and she darted out of the way. Urban shoved it to the side, and they stood together to ensure the demon perished. Once it quit thrashing, the Mist did its thing, transcending the remains into the Gloom. Live demons couldn't run around long before the realm expelled them.

To be sure, she looked over her shoulder. A furtive move that was becoming second nature. Once she started doing it, she recalled countless times she'd witnessed warriors in the realm do the same. A quick look around. A casual scan. Moments when their gazes flitted left, then right.

She was becoming one of them.

They'd been hunting for a few nights, taking only symasters and a pair of sylphs that had made the mistake of traveling in such a small group. Urban had done the fighting, and she'd been the angel-fire wielder. She wasn't desensitized, but each time was easier. Her hands had already quit shaking.

"Good job." Urban glanced down at himself. Symaster blood stained his clothing, and his boots were coated with guts. He wiped the gore off on the thick grass under their feet.

The longer she was here, the less she was weirded out by the place. It wasn't a place of peace—it just existed—but there was a sense of peace in that. A place that had nothing to prove but to be itself.

"Ready to call it a night?" he asked. They'd been returning to the safe house, changing and cleaning up, and then going back out. Nothing had happened between them since their time in the garage. She was getting restless.

"Yes." Their car was still at the casino. They'd have to catch a ride in the light of day and find another place to hunt.

He cocked an elbow. They didn't have to hang on to each other, but entering the realm ensured they'd arrive together instead of transcending into the other person. She'd full-body smashed into Urban the other night, not in a good way.

She was growing restless. When they weren't out hunting, Urban made her sit around her bedroom with her wings out since she wasn't used to a long-term morph. He updated his boss, checked in with his team, and they slept —in separate rooms. The last few days, he'd been nothing more than her mentor, and everything about that was grating on her nerves.

She wasn't ready to claim eternity with him, but it'd be

nice to rely on him. Not as her savior. Not as her teacher. Not even as a buddy who exchanged bad jokes with her. She wanted him to herself. She wanted to be something to someone.

Maybe he was ashamed of her? She dwelled on the thought as she hooked her arm through his and stepped through the Mist and into the dry air of Nevada. Urban opened the door for her and she entered. He took his shoes off and treaded in behind her.

"Remember to let your wings out after your shower. Maybe even sleep with them out."

The house had light-blocking blinds, and Urban had put a blanket over her window to make sure no one could peep around the edges if they were able to scale the fence into the yard.

"Sure." Another night was done, and he'd go his separate way, to use the bathroom on the first floor and then go up to his room and not speak to her. Another night when she wouldn't bring up what had happened between them. How many more times would they do this? How long before she started thinking of the way he got her off as a dream, something she'd imagined?

And then what would she do? She stalled before climbing the stairs. Would she settle and take what she was offered just like she had growing up? She hadn't demanded her parents act better toward her. She hadn't expected more of herself. Would she let another important part of her life make her feel insignificant and quietly change her ways and what she expected of herself?

No. She turned, catching Urban before he disappeared into the bathroom. The small laundry closet was across from the bathroom, but he never stripped in the hallway, like she might get the wrong impression. She didn't want to guess.

She was tired of the game. "I'll take a nice long shower in case you finish early and want to join me." He froze, his back ramrod straight. "Just know that if I finish my shower, get out, dry off, let my wings free, and climb into bed and I don't see you, I'll write off the other night as a fluke that you regret." He opened his mouth, but she held up a hand. "Regardless of whether you regret it, I'll take it as your way of saying you don't want more between us. Since you haven't said otherwise, I need to make sure we're clear on this. I'll be training and moving on with my life, and I'm not holding myself back for anyone anymore."

With that, she jogged up the stairs and went to her bedroom.

CHAPTER 10

Urban didn't intend to take the fastest shower of his life. He had demon remains on himself, and he needed to make sure they all got cleaned off. He also needed to think. She'd kicked open the figurative door and told him exactly when it would shut. What she'd really told him was to make up his mind.

He'd been indecisive, and he had to figure out why. He was her mentor, sure. But she was ready for training. And then he'd be a fully trained and experienced warrior and she'd just be starting out. Numen warriors didn't have ranks like human military. The *Don't be a dick* saying went a long way. A full warrior dating a trainee wasn't unusual. In fact, they all fucked around a lot. Numen could live long lives and were hard to kill. So working in a field where they witnessed other long-lived beings die horribly painful deaths reminded them of their own mortality. Their lives weren't short—but they could be.

A lot of Numen attributed their fucking around to fearing a sync mate. They wanted to fit as much sex in before they were destined to one mate. That wasn't the only reason—they were more than selfish libidos—but add in the lingering adrenaline surge after a fight, and yeah, warriors liked to mess around.

All those reasons weren't pertinent right now. He didn't want to fail Persephone. She'd been let down by the two people who should've held her up the highest. She was trying to make up for the way she'd let others down. And he didn't want to interfere with her healing.

But the female he'd fought with had jumped a ton of obstacles. She wasn't hindered, and all he was doing was creating an obstacle in her mind. Did he want her or not?

He wanted nothing but her. So maybe it was time she knew it. He'd have to be honest, though. He didn't want her to get the wrong idea about how much he wanted to be with her, but he couldn't let her think he was the type to want a mate.

He finished in the bathroom. When he walked out, the washing machine was whirring away and the shower was running upstairs.

Good. He wasn't late. He had nothing but a towel around his waist, but he yanked it off and tossed it on top of the washer.

Her bedroom door wasn't locked. He'd never tried it. She'd probably never locked it, waiting for him to get over himself and come to her.

Inside, a slit of light escaped from the ajar bathroom door. He strode for it before he started questioning whether this was the best thing for him or her.

Her back was to him. His gaze licked over the mottled skin, angry lines lighter than her unburned skin. She pushed her hair off her face and let the spray rain down on her; the line she cut was stunning. Erotic. Rounded ass. A peek of her full breasts on each side.

It wasn't until he pulled open the shower door that she

noticed him. "You need more situational awareness," he said around a thick throat. It was amazing he could speak. All the blood had left his brain. She was gorgeous, but he'd never witnessed her nude, and the sight robbed him of words.

She turned, and his mouth grew dry. High tits, soft abdomen with ridges of hard muscle underneath, and hips curving to legs he couldn't wait to have wrapped around his head. He took it all in, and his mouth went from parched to watering to get a taste of her.

"I didn't think you were coming." She held herself back, like she was worried he'd walk right out.

"The other night wasn't a fluke. I want you—so fucking bad. But, Persephone, I'm a not-forever guy. I'm not ready to mate and settle down."

"I'm not either."

"You're not a female who's going to bang through training and hook up after a big battle."

She shook her head. "I'm not. But is it so bad if you're the one I want to bang?"

His cock twitched like it was demanding to know why they hadn't gotten to the fun part yet. "I just want the air cleared. What we're doing. I like being around you. I want to know what it's like to be inside you. But the idea of a mate? That's not for me."

"Okay. I've been warned. We're just seeing what it's like to date and stuff, and I want to get to that 'stuff' really bad." She pressed her back to the wall. Were doubts about her scars suddenly slamming into her?

Fuck that. "Turn around."

Her eyes flared, but her mouth tightened like she knew he saw right through her. He didn't. He saw her. Period.

He put his hands on her hips and briefly closed his eyes. How easy it would be to lift her so she'd twine those strong legs around him. He'd sink into her heat and get her to come before he spilled inside her.

No. She was his for the rest of the night. If she didn't know she was ready for full training, she would when they returned to Numen in the morning. He'd already sent Director Vale the message in case he was tempted to stay in the safe house and have her to himself for days.

He opened his eyes, and whatever she saw in his gaze made her breath hitch. She flicked her tongue out to lick her bottom lip. He smashed his mouth to hers and caught it, letting her heat seep into him, her flavor. She momentarily tensed, then relaxed.

Perfect. He wanted to keep kissing her, but there'd be time for that. He wanted nothing between them, including her doubts.

Pulling away, he spun her. She was tense by the time she was completely turned around.

"Do they still hurt?" He'd quit asking her after she'd chewed him out in the training room, but that didn't mean he wasn't constantly wondering.

"Mostly when I wake up. They ache during the day, but I'm getting used to it."

He traced the largest of the scars around her shoulder blades. His team hadn't gotten to her in time. A few drops had hit her and burned through her clothing before chewing away at her skin. If she'd gotten the full vial, she'd be gone. So much damage that she would've been unable to heal herself.

But she was here. When he stared at the smaller scars, she shivered.

"You feel that more?" he asked.

She nodded.

He ran his hands down the space where her wings would be if they were out. "I'm shutting the water off.

We're drying off, then I want you to let your wings out and lie on the bed. I want you spread before me like a five-course meal."

She nodded.

He flipped the faucet off and got the towels. He couldn't look at her while he was drying himself off. His erection was painful and straining for her.

She was toweling off her hair, and her breasts were jiggling.

Change of plans. He tossed his towel onto the counter and drew her toward him. "I just need a taste." He dipped his head to run his tongue over one nipple before drawing it into his mouth.

She groaned and stuffed her fingers into his damp hair. "I'm not dry yet."

"I don't want you dry," he growled. "I want you wet." He was about to pick her up by putting an arm behind her knees and an arm around her back, but he caught himself in time. No pain tonight. "Lie on the bed."

She scurried out of the bathroom.

"Wings," he reminded her.

He didn't see her close her eyes, but she unmorphed her wings. She unfurled them slowly, deliberately, but it wasn't a sexual display. She could no longer whip out her wings without considering the pull on her scars. When she was fully released, she took a breath.

Her blankets were all over the place. His angel didn't like to make the bed apparently. She flipped the bedding back and stretched out on the burgundy sheets. He was about to ask whether the position on her back hurt, but she'd never confess if it did.

If she was feeling any aches or pain, he'd override the discomfort with unadulterated pleasure.

"Spread your legs." He prowled toward her. She'd

revealed his own personal heaven by the time he wedged his shoulders between her thighs. Her pewter wings rested out to the sides, the perfect frame for her body. And at the junction between her legs, she was glistening for him, and it wasn't from the shower.

He'd been trying not to imagine that view for so long that he had to take a moment. "Even better than my dreams."

He licked through her seam, tasting the sweetness that was her.

She moaned, and her legs fell farther open. "Urban."

Everything in her tone told him it'd been so long for her. For him too. But he also heard that what experiences she'd had, they'd fallen below expectations. He'd surpass them.

He circled her clit with his tongue, swept through her folds, and speared into her. She arched off the bed with a needy moan. "Do it again."

He did. Over and over until she was writhing. Then he concentrated on her clit and threaded a finger into her. She immediately started riding him. He brought her to the brink and pulled back, slowly pushing in a second finger.

"Yes," she whined. Instead of grasping at the sheets, she gripped his hair and rode him. This time, he gave it to her.

She was allowed to be loud. After months of talking and telling jokes, trying to be as quiet as possible, he'd never tire of hearing her voice bounce off the walls.

Her body clenched around his fingers, and the ripples of her muscles milked him. Fuck, she was going to kill him when he finally got inside her; it'd be the best death ever.

When she sagged into the mattress, he rose to his knees. His cock pounded to the beat of his heart, slamming within his chest. "Roll over."

She frowned and looked around as if wondering what was wrong.

"I'm going to fuck you from behind, where I get a full view of your scars, so you have no doubt they don't bother me."

Desire flared hot in her eyes, but uncertainty lingered like a stain he needed to wash away. "You don't have to—"

"Roll over, Persephone."

She pulled her knees up and to the side. He got the best show as she rolled to her hands and knees, her wings brushing along his skin and tickling over his dick until he thought he'd explode all over her backside.

The thought made him freeze. "I need a condom. Fuck. I need a condom."

She looked over her shoulder again, her damp hair hanging down while her ass was in the air. She was right there, on the edge of his cock, but he didn't move.

"We don't get pregnant that easily." The need clogging her voice drove him wild, but he couldn't.

"But what if?"

She thought for a moment. "Quit worrying and get inside me."

He kicked his hips forward before his brain caught up. It was hardly a worry—Numen rarely used condoms—but the decision was ultimately hers. As soon as the tip of his cock hit her sweltering heat, he was lost. He sank in all the way and gripped her hips. A long groan left him as he rocked gently, letting her get used to him and allowing himself to gain control of himself, so he didn't blow in seconds.

When she bowed her back and her wings fluttered wider, he couldn't restrain himself any longer. He thrust. And again. She met him each time. The sound of their skin slapping together filled the room. Her wings tensed, as tight as the rest of her. She was coiling again, readying for another explosion. So fucking close to coming. Her ass in the air, presented to him. He watched himself slide in and out of her over and over again.

"Urban." She was reaching her precipice, and he wanted them to come together. He wanted to feel her shatter around him, milking him the way she had his fingers.

He leaned over her and wrapped an arm around her. He found her clit again, and without losing momentum, he got her all the way to her peak.

"Yes! Urban… Yes."

He thrust as lightning raced down his spine, making his balls impossibly tighter. Then the storm inside him broke. "Fuck!" He bucked against her, propping himself on his hands. She was quivering under him but still moving with him.

They were good together. In so many ways. He was daunted by how much she meant to him.

No, it was the sex muddling his brain. He cared for her, but he wouldn't fall in love. Love wasn't for warriors, no matter how many of his teammates succumbed.

He eased out of her, rubbing his hands down her ass. He could go again in a minute if she were ready, but mostly, he wanted to cuddle her. They didn't have long together, and maybe this was the only time they'd have for a while. He was a warrior. He'd been actively shunning mates for decades, but tonight, he'd hold her.

PERSEPHONE AWOKE to Urban massaging her back. They'd roused hours ago, but she'd still been sore from all the sex. He'd made her sleep longer.

"Ready?" he asked.

"Mmm." No. Maybe. She hugged her pillow and enjoyed the way he was awakening the skin on her back, preparing it to move and stretch after rest. She was ready to start full training, but she didn't want to leave the bed with Urban. "What happens when we return?"

"I'm talking to the director when we get back. I'll let you know. But you're going to train with Stana. She's got Kadee, Mac, and Molly in her group."

Her happiness soared. "Really?"

His smile was indulgent. "I told him you were a fast learner and could catch up and that being with them would benefit all of you."

"Wow, thank you." A moment of doubt hounded her. "Do you think I'd struggle without them?"

"No. But I think you four are the making of a team, and if you train together, it'll make you all stronger. Trust is the foundation of a solid team."

She rolled over and ran her hand over his jaw. His profile was strong. Hard. But his eyes were soft. She'd noticed the tenderness when he began visiting her bedroom after her accident, but she hadn't dared hope he had feelings. "I don't want to have to sneak around. If you want to keep seeing others—"

He put a finger over her lips. "No, I don't. But we're not sneaking around. If we have to wait until training's done, so be it."

She nodded and wrapped her fingers around his, then moved his hand from her mouth. She could climb on top of him again, but she wouldn't. It was time to go. Time to move into another phase of her life. She refused to be scared.

He got off the bed. She cleaned up, dressed in the clothing she usually wore for training, and met him at the back porch.

When they ascended to a spot outside the barracks, she smiled at him. The same fresh air greeted her. Old marble buildings towered over them. Voices drifted in the air from the training grounds. "I guess this is it."

"You know where to find Stana's section?"

She nodded. Stana was three inches shorter than her and walked like she was ready to punch out the entire realm. The female was intimidating, but instead of being fearful, Persephone grew more excited. If she could learn a shred of the warrior's badassery, she'd be happy. "Have a good talk."

Urban's gaze dipped to her mouth, but he held himself with his usual rigidity. He was back to being a warrior instead of her lover. Couldn't he be both?

"I'll miss you," she said as she walked away.

"I hope I gave you enough to remember me until next time."

She was still smiling after she cleared the barracks and found the large open training field. The grass was perpetually thick, no matter how much of a beating it took from the training warriors. Stana spotted her and pointed to the end of a long line of trainees. In the group, she found her friends.

Persephone jogged to her place, and during the next four hours, she worked harder than she ever had. It was exhilarating, and no matter how much her back ached or how bleak her little cot in the barracks seemed after being in bed with Urban, nothing could take away her accomplishments.

After the trainees were dismissed for the evening, Kadee beelined for her. "What was it like?"

"Scary," she answered honestly. "The first time Urban wanted me to use angel fire, I froze."

Kadee giggled. "Oh, man. Was he upset?"

Molly fell in step with them.

Mac pulled up alongside, his right wing hitched higher than the other. His left side must've been hurting, but he didn't let it show. "I doubt it. Did you see the way his gaze stripped her down and devoured her?"

Persephone gasped. "He did not—You didn't see that, did you?"

Mac smirked. "Urban isn't used to sneaky Numen like me. Yes. You two couldn't hide that there's something between you." He lifted his chin to Kadee. "You owe me a bushel of Gala apples."

"Why apples?"

Kadee made a frustrated noise. "Because I'd have to haul them from the market all the way here."

"No, 'cause she'll have to haggle with the fruit vendor who tallies everyone's purchases. He hates making trips to the human realm and hauling fruit back."

"He's been a bear since his daughter's gone to the human realm," Kadee said.

"Elodie's been acting so different since her boyfriend died," Molly added. "I heard her mom tell mine she was worried about her. I feel so bad."

"She's still gone?" Persephone remembered when Tommy was killed. Elodie and Tommy were close to her age, but they were good people and had steered clear of Persephone. A wise choice since Persephone would've constantly pointed out their different stations in life. And when the two had started dating, Persephone had thought they made an odd pair. They'd been good friends, but lovers? Then Persephone had gotten hurt, and she'd forgotten as many people as had forgotten her.

Her parents had been muttering about the young couple outside her door, but when she tried to roll out of bed to eavesdrop, they'd scurried away. She'd been so irritated at herself for not moving faster, so impatient with the healing process. Then she'd recalled what they said about Tommy. *Persephone still has her life, while Senator Thomas lost his grandson.* As if it was proof of how unfair things could be. As if Persephone wasn't already feeling like the realm's biggest waste of time.

That conversation was also when something inside her had shifted permanently. She wanted to help people like Tommy—people who were caught off guard by demons and their lives destroyed. She didn't want to wander Numen, muttering, "What a shame…"

"She's gone," Mac said, pulling Persephone from her thoughts. "Her house is locked up tight, and her dad is cranky as hell. Kind of like your warrior when he was trying to act like he didn't want to get into your robes."

Persephone playfully scowled at him. "I haven't worn robes since I got here."

The group moved around the building, and Mac patted her on the shoulder, careful not to slap her wings. "Speak, and he shall appear."

Her gaze landed on Urban. The others filed into the building while she crossed to Urban. Her heart pounded. She couldn't tell from his expression, but he was adept at hiding his feelings—unless someone like Mac was nosing around.

She crossed her arms like she could give herself a hug. "If it's bad news, just come out with it."

His features softened, but his warrior hardness was still in place. "It's not terrible. He's asked us to keep it professional until you're done with training. And then we'll be like the rest of the warriors who can date."

She frowned. No, the news wasn't terrible, but she'd be in training in the realm for a month and then in the field for another month. After that, she'd be considered a rookie for at least a year. "Training, or until I'm a full warrior?"

His mouth curved in a wry smile. "Full warrior." He leaned closer, but to others, they'd look like they were in an intense conversation, not on the brink of kissing. "Although there's a three-day break between the training on the grounds and field training."

A smile played along her lips. "I don't know… I might be busy."

His expression turned serious again. "Director Vale did ask where you planned to stay after you're done with training."

Her parents hadn't talked to her since that day in the workout room. "I'll have to find a small place." She'd be making her own money soon after.

"Just something to think about. You have a few months."

"Will I get to see you before my month of training is up?"

His face fell, and he shook his head. "No. I have to go to Earth to aid my team on a mission that might…" His gaze traveled around them. "It's important, and they need all hands on deck."

"Be careful."

"Always." He took a deliberate step back. "You'll do fine." Another step back. "In fact, I think you're going to be one of the best."

He turned and walked away. He could've said anything to her.

You can do it.

Hang in there.

I'll be thinking about you.

But he'd built her up—and given her a hell of a compliment. She nearly floated into the barracks.

CHAPTER 11

The clear Montana air was getting cooler. Fall was closer, and while the days were still warm, the nights dipped lower. Ransom and Sierra wore sweaters and jeans. Boone had gone inside to put Arik down for the night. Urban was quiet in a chair next to Sierra, but he'd been quiet since he returned from Numen to work with the team. Sandeen was getting the firepit going, and Harlowe was helping him, but they weren't there to party.

Tonight was for decisions. After two weeks of spinning their wheels, the team was no further along following the signs that another female had been taken or that more were being trafficked. Sandeen spent his days scouring the Gloom since that was as far as any angels could get to the underworld. He might control the mines and be a powerful demon in his birth realm, but the half angel wasn't the guy other demons shared secrets with.

So tonight was for strategizing. Brainstorming. Dionna, Bronx, and Jagger were working in Numen, searching that end for any information, but what they really needed was an informant.

"I could be a decoy," Elodie said. She abruptly sat forward in her camp chair. All they needed were long sticks and marshmallows and they'd look like a group of humans enjoying the Montana wilderness instead of discussing how to infiltrate a trafficking ring of angels and demons.

Ransom didn't like the words that left Elodie's mouth. "No."

Sandeen held up a hand. "Wait. That's not a bad idea. No one knows you're here, they definitely don't know you know us, but they're suspicious of you. What are you thinking?" He had no protective stance where Elodie was concerned, which made him more objective…and even more of an asshole for hearing her out.

The fire flickered in her uncertain eyes. "I don't know. Whoever *they* are will want to get rid of me if they think I know something. They don't know you've found me. If I return to Numen, they won't think any of you found me—but they'll still want me gone. Maybe I can lure whoever it is to me, and if I'm taken, Sierra could track where I'm at."

Harlowe crossed her booted feet. "These people have a small but powerful ring. They're familiar with us and who we deal with in the realm, and they're careful not to do their business with anyone associated with us. So as long as Elodie isn't seen around us, it's a good idea, an excellent one. The only other option is someone we can plant in the senate—someone we trust."

"Which highlights my initial concern," Elodie said. "No one in the realm knows about what's going on unless they're fighting against it or doing these malicious acts."

No matter what, it'd get complicated. Ransom glanced around the faces circling the campfire and landed on Urban. He was scowling into the flames, his brow furrowed. Was he even thinking about the mission? Or was he still obsessed with whatever had dominated his mind since he'd returned?

"Urban?" he asked. "Got any ideas?"

"What about the Nassims?" Harlowe asked. "They trust us, and we trust them. Aren't they upset Persephone's going through warrior training? Can we use that?"

Urban's glare shot to her. The muscle in his jaw flexed, and he directed his gaze back to the flames. "We aren't fucking using her."

"Care to share why?" Sandeen asked, unafraid of being nosy.

"If I was her, I'd want retribution on the assholes behind an attack on me," Harlowe said in a way meant to prod Urban.

"They're dead."

Sierra's steady gaze was on Urban. "If you have anything pertinent to tell us, perhaps you should spill it. Personal secrets only get used against the team."

Urban's scowl deepened. "Are you trying to get me to tell everyone I spent a week in a safe house with Persephone to get her ready for training?"

Sierra just cocked a brow.

Ransom should've stayed out of it, but it grated that Urban was reluctant to offer information on a female whose parents might be able to help them while saying nothing when Elodie said she could be bait.

Harlowe nudged Sandeen with an elbow. "Florida."

"Right." Sandeen tilted his head. "What exactly were you making sure this Persephone was ready for?"

"We needed to know she was mentally prepared to wield angel fire," Urban said, stubbornness in his tone.

"So you're not banging her?" Sandeen asked, a gotcha smile playing along his lips.

Urban snarled and rose to pace behind the chairs.

"Whatever's going on there, it's private." He shot Sierra a determined look. "And it's not a secret. I've already talked to the director."

"Okay," Ransom said. "So why can't we ask her to help us with her parents?"

"They're closer to the director than her," Urban explained. "They're closer to his mate and Senator Felicia than her. We know the people we're after will steer clear of Felicia, but the Nassims' relationship with the director and the females is well known. They won't get any further than Felicia."

"Are we sure we can trust the Nassims?" Sandeen asked.

"They were our only support before Felicia became a senator," Harlowe said. "If they were up to something, some of us would be dead by now. They're good people, and after what happened to Persephone, I can't imagine how worried they are about her."

Sierra's expression softened. "There are worse things than having a worried parent."

Ransom's heart didn't warm as much as it should've. They were left, then, with Elodie's plan. "I don't want Elodie in harm's way. We've got to figure out a different way."

"No." Elodie reached over to squeeze his hand, giving him a regretful smile. But the determination in her gaze never wavered. "I can't stay away from Numen forever, nor can I hide on Earth and do nothing. I want to help. I want to get the people who killed Tommy. If I return and act like something's bothering me, act like I know something no one else does—which won't be hard—I'll be like a pot of honey to all the vile bees."

He didn't care if he had witnesses to his worry. Someone had to be the voice of reason. "You can't be a target. I know we've been training, but there might be more than one involved. They might not send just one person after you, and they might have training too."

Elodie rubbed her hands like she was trying to keep warm, like the chill of danger went right through her. "I have to try. As much as I'm learning here with you, others are in danger. What if the creatures in the underworld succeeded with that female? What if the blood is from a baby being born? There might be more than one innocent life at stake. I can't not do anything. I'm going back."

He wanted to wrap his arms around her. "I'll go with you."

She shook her head. "They can't know about me and all of you."

He wasn't going to drop it. "But we have to communicate. I can get into your place without being seen, and I'll just stay there." The offer sounded like a weak excuse to keep close to her, and yeah, there was that too. But he couldn't risk her. "No one will know you're not going home alone."

Was that relief crossing her face? It was one thing to hunt in the human realm. To learn to defend herself. But another to walk into a web when she didn't know who any of the spiders were.

Sierra crossed one leg over the other. "It'll be nice to get the rot out of the senate."

Elodie nodded, but her gaze turned speculative. "If we can weed out the evil and make a more transparent senate, what do you propose should be done with fallen?"

"I don't know," Sierra said. "All I know is that I'd feel better if no one in Numen knows about Boone and Arik, not until our son is an adult at least."

Guilt crossed Elodie's face. "The family of fallen shouldn't be shut out of their lives forever."

"No," Sierra agreed. "But I have no one left in Numen." She tipped her head toward Ransom. "I have my father."

Elodie exchanged a grateful glance with him that hid another emotion he couldn't identify. "I guess I do too now."

～

URBAN STOOD in front of the simple house on the corner of a quiet street close to the angel-fire fountain in the middle of Numen. His mother walked outside, squinted into the sun, then did a double take. "Urban?"

She looked older than when he'd seen her last—not an easy feat for a Numen. Her hair was dark like his, long but frizzier than before, as if the ends had been broken off at random lengths.

"Mother."

"What's wrong?"

His heart sank. He never came around, so of course she'd think something was wrong. Perhaps it was. A comment Sierra had made when part of his team had come up with a plan for Elodie had sat in his gut like a crooked lead weight. *There are worse things than having a worried parent.*

His parents hadn't been great, but the statement had him wondering if he'd been too superficial. If he'd seen his parents' fights as a rejection of himself instead of just two people who shouldn't have been paired together.

"Nothing. It's been a while since we talked."

"Well, I was just heading to the market, but that can wait. Want to come inside?"

He nodded and followed her in.

The tidy house held nothing but cozy furniture. Vibrant colors on the walls and woven into the rugs.

Mother's house was bright and feminine. Nothing like when he'd grown up. There were no signs of his father or the cigars from Earth he liked to smoke.

"Does Father ever…" What? Visit? Come home? Was this even his home anymore?

She looked at him like he'd asked about a ghost. "Why would he come around?"

They were mates. "I didn't know that you two were completely cut off."

She shrugged. "He said he wanted nothing to do with me."

He'd said that to Urban too. Guess he'd meant it.

She settled on a settee, letting her light-gray wings hang behind her. She stretched her legs out and crossed them at the ankles. "So, what really brought you by?"

His mother had always been no nonsense. Was that why she'd taken Father's abandonment so well? Urban needed answers. He had three days coming up with a female he was quickly growing too fond of and he couldn't be fighting his emotions while he desperately just wanted to sink into her body.

"There's this girl—"

"Almighty, Urban. You want to mate someone?"

Of all the people he could be honest with, he didn't expect it to be his mother. "Maybe someday."

"Mating your father ruined my damn life."

He gave her a steady look. "How, exactly?"

She held up her wrist, the one with the single-wing sync brand received when a Numen was paired with someone. Their mate wore the other half of the wings. "This. Took me away from a really great guy. I went to save your father's ass, trusted that my mate was the best for me, and now here I am. Alone."

"You were seeing someone?"

"Then I was," she said flippantly. "Now I'm seeing a few someones."

More than he needed to know, but then his father was likely seeing a few someones right now too. "Would you have mated that male you were seeing before the sync brand?"

She lifted a shoulder. "Maybe. Knowing what I know now? No."

"What do you know now?"

"That mating ruined every relationship I had. Look how your father turned you against me."

"What do you mean?"

"You left as soon as you were old enough. Followed in his footsteps as a warrior. You sure don't come to see me."

He didn't, but she blamed Father for that too. "It was both of you. The fighting."

"There you go. Mating ruins everything."

It was a mantra he'd heard much of throughout his formative years. "Why mating, though? You're living the life you'd want to live. You have the mating bond you're ignoring. So what's different?"

She leaned forward, her eyes narrowed. "The difference is being thoroughly rejected by someone the Almighty deemed worthy of you. The difference is being looked at like you stole someone's breath when it was your healing ability that gave them life. The difference is that in the end, mating bond and this damn mark, I'm still alone. I have a mate I never see and a child who's going to blame me for being clear about how a sync bond ruined my life."

This visit was a worse idea the longer he was here. "Why did you mate him, though? You could've saved him and gone about your life."

"Who's going to take me with someone else's mark?" She shook her head and sighed. "Like I always said, it's better to be single. You won't have to break some nice guy's heart when you get this damn mark. You won't have to risk rejection if you do mate. And you won't find yourself telling your kid that your relationship with him was ruined because of some selfish male."

What about her role in their relationship? But the last thing sticking in his mind was that it was better to be single.

PERSEPHONE WALKED BACK to the barracks with her friends. Real friends. Each day she awoke, she looked forward to training. Anticipated the ass-chewing Stana was likely to give them for being too slow, too clumsy, or too distracted. The four weeks were intense, but they made progress in leaps and bounds.

Kadee yawned next to her. "I'm going to pass out before I take my first bite."

"I'm already asleep." Mac rolled his shoulders. "Stana was especially wicked today. I think I might be falling for her."

Molly's boisterous laugh rang out. "She'd chew you up and spit you out. But truth? I think you have a shot when you go to a real team after our month in the field."

Mac's face lit up. "Really?"

"Stana likes to play, is what I've heard." Molly nudged Persephone. "I know you don't gossip anymore, but come on. You had to have heard something."

"Believe it or not, I never paid attention to warrior gossip." She dropped her voice to a scandalous whisper. "It was beneath my station."

"Ooh," Kadee said. "I think that's even more scandalous."

"It's what I used to aim for," Persephone said, some of her humor evaporating.

It hurt less to be reminded of how she used to be, but a familiar figure dipped down from the sky to land by the headquarters building in front of their barracks, distracting her from the remaining pain.

Her decision was immediate. "Hey, don't wait for me. There's someone I need to talk to."

Kadee followed her gaze and hissed, "You can't just go accost the director's mate." She blinked. "Oh, maybe you can."

"My accosting days are done." She jogged off, her legs tired but still full of energy. A sure sign her training had done its job.

Odessa had disappeared around the corner of the building where the front entrance was. Persephone had to catch her before the female went inside, otherwise her courage might fade.

"Odessa, wait."

Odessa turned, her expression curious, until it landed on Persephone. Then anxiety scrawled across her face before she squared her shoulders and schooled her features. "Persephone. Hello."

Persephone hated that the female still had that reaction around her. "Sorry to bother you." Surprise flitted across the female's face, and yeah, Persephone hadn't been one for apologies—about anything—before her injuries. "I, um... I wanted to tell you how sorry I am for the way I treated you. I was awful."

Odessa shifted her stance. Her wings dipped a moment, then rose. Familiar jealousy curled through Persephone's belly. The female was gorgeous. Wide crystalline blue-green eyes. Long hair cascading down her back. She wore a simple white robe that fell to her shins, but she made it look like a ball gown.

"You were awful." She feathered her fingers over her collar. "You know what? I really needed that apology. I've come so far, but I've been scared of running across you every time I come to see Bryant. Felicia said she talked to you and that you were different, but…" She shook her head.

"I was too horrible to believe, it's true. And I shouldn't get off so easy just because I got a few scars."

Odessa's smile was understanding. "I don't wish your injuries on anyone, but I do admire what you're doing with your life. Being a warrior isn't easy, and I understand your mother is less than pleased."

"They've never had faith in me."

Odessa tilted her head. "What do you mean?"

"Isn't it obvious?"

The female frowned. "No. They've always spoken well of you. I mean, they were worried. And I could tell they were disappointed with how you used to act, but they love you. That's clear."

"Is it?" Persephone didn't know what else to say. She hadn't heard about this side of her parents, and she certainly hadn't seen it. "They doted on you and Felicia, and I felt like they hung you both over my head as an ideal I could never attain but one they wanted so badly for me."

Sympathy entered Odessa's bright gaze. "I'm sorry that's how they made you feel." Her smile was small. "I admit after losing my mother and my father turning distant, I craved your parents' attention. I would've done anything to make them proud."

"I couldn't seem to make them proud, so I didn't do anything." She shared a supportive look with Odessa.

"Well, if that wasn't a lot of years wasted being a bitch when you would've been an amazing friend."

Odessa chuckled. "We're young yet. Perhaps we could get to know each other—as we are now, not as we were then."

And perhaps Persephone should give her parents the same consideration. They needed to get to know her as she was, not who they thought she was. Then perhaps they wouldn't be as worried about her being a warrior.

With enough effort, she could get over the hurt they'd caused and forgive them. Same for them.

The front doors opened, and the director's large frame blocked the entrance. "Ah, I was just coming to look for you."

"I was chatting with one of your newest warriors." Odessa grinned. "I don't think I've truly met her before."

"Careful," the director said as he came down the stairs. "She'll surprise you."

"She certainly has."

Persephone stepped back. "I've taken enough of your time, and I've got to eat and prepare for tomorrow's training."

"Then you have leave." Director Vale's statement was direct. She did have leave, and he knew what she planned to do with it.

"Yes. I can't wait. And I think… I might talk to my parents too."

His usually hard expression softened on his unscarred side. "Good idea. Then they can get off my arse."

Odessa set her hand on the director's shoulder. "Parents worry. You'll have to get used to it."

It took a moment for her words to sink in. Persephone gasped, genuinely thrilled for a female she used to envy. "You're expecting? Congratulations!"

The director's eyes shone in a way Persephone didn't think was possible for such a hard man. "Thank you," he said gruffly. "Now get some chow, and don't tell everyone. I can't stand the dopey grins they get when they look at me."

Laughing, Persephone left the couple, marveling over how their lives were changing and for the better. She'd use the improvement to brave her parents.

CHAPTER 12

Urban waited outside Persephone's barracks. The talk with his mom had done nothing but bang around in his head. Persephone had three days of leave before she had to go to the earthly realm, and he was left wondering if his mother was right. Was it better to stay single? But then she was messing around with a few individuals, if she could be believed. He didn't doubt it, though.

He knew damn well his mother had meant to stay unattached. And he'd tried to do the same. Wall off his heart. And he was still single. He didn't want to mess around with anyone other than Persephone, but… What if? What if he got critically injured and he was assigned a mate to help save him and it wasn't her? What the hell would he do?

And what if she got terribly injured and some asshole got her sync mark?

Rage swept through him so hot he thought it must be what the underworld felt like.

She breezed out of the building, her tinkling laughter falling like crystal raindrops on his ears. She spotted him, and her eyes lit up.

Fuck, he felt like a bastard. He couldn't put on a full smile, but the corner of his mouth tipped up. Kadee was with her. She squeezed Persephone's arm. "See ya in a few days."

"I'll be right here, bags packed." Persephone scooted close to him, a sultry smile on her face. "Hey there."

"Hey."

Her grin dropped. "What's wrong?"

"Nothing." Her expression said she wasn't buying it, so he shrugged. "I visited my mother, and I shouldn't have."

"That bad?"

"Not good." He started walking, wishing he could do something he'd never really done before—hold hands. His emotions were raw, and his brain was telling him to keep his distance, but the tightness in his chest suggested holding Persephone would make him feel better.

"And here I was wondering if I shouldn't talk to my parents."

"Why?" He stopped because he had no idea where to go. She didn't have a place in the realm, and his house was little better than a plain hotel room. It was merely a place to sleep and shower.

A line formed between her brows. "I talked to Odessa."

"How'd that go?" Persephone hadn't spared anyone her snide remarks, but Odessa had gotten the biggest dose.

"Well, surprisingly, really well, but only because she's just as amazing as my parents always said."

"You're amazing too."

Her smile was sweet. "I wasn't always, but it made me think that my parents and I are stuck in this stasis of old judgments and maybe I should be the bigger person and give them another chance."

He'd given his mother another chance, and they'd stayed in their stasis, but Persephone was younger than him. She was smart enough, confident enough, to know she didn't need her parents, but she also craved their attention, their love.

The idea of craving love settled deep in Urban's gut. He'd grown up in a cold house. He watched humans do awful things, with or without demon interference. At times, he went to his own cold house and wished there was…more there. He couldn't identify what more meant.

But this wasn't about him. "I think you should. Do it before you go into the field again."

"Urban—our days together."

He wanted to be around her forever, but the fact was her parents were a constant in her life. He wasn't. If she could find new ground with them, she'd have them with her forever. He'd be out doing his job and going home alone. "We can still be together, but this is important. I think you should stay with them for leave." It gutted him to tell her to stay somewhere without him, but he'd seen how hard it was for her with her parents. If they could repair the bridge between them, she'd want time. "I can still visit, like we used to."

He almost missed those days. Not her pain or her sorrow. He missed when they could just be in the dark without witnesses. He was Urban, she was Persephone, and they were nothing else.

"You need a place to stay during leave anyway," he said.

Confusion lit her brown eyes, and he realized she'd been expecting to be with him for the full three days, just like he'd planned to be inside her for that long. The month without her had been hard enough. What would his life be like after three days with her and then nothing? He'd be the same as his house. An empty space to exist.

No. No, he couldn't play house with this female.

She pulled her lower lip into her mouth, and he forced himself to stay rooted in place when he wanted to capture that lip with his mouth instead. "What if…we all got together, like a meal or something?" She shook her head. "I'm getting ahead of myself. They might run me off."

"They won't. They need tough love, but they'll see how wonderful you are." He put his hands on either side of her shoulders. "And yes, I'll come over for a meal if they're willing to let me through the door. This is important to you, so it's important to me."

He thought she'd melt into him and they'd have their first semipublic embrace. He feared it as much as he anticipated it.

Instead, she searched his face. "Is everything okay?"

When in doubt, default to work. "It's the mission we're working on."

"There's more trouble in the realm?"

Of course she'd guess he wasn't assigned to just any warrior task. He was part of the director's special team. "I can't say."

"Does it have anything to do with Elodie Rogers?"

"How do you know of her?"

"So it does?"

Shit. Another reason he needed to put more distance between them. He was slipping. Even when she became a full warrior, he wouldn't be able to tell her everything.

However, Boone and Sierra were a team. Same with Felicia and Jagger. He doubted the director kept anything from Odessa, and Sandeen was mischievous, but he'd taken everything Harlowe told him to the grave and beyond. Hell, Bronx probably poured his heart out to Tosca.

But he wasn't mated to Persephone, and he didn't plan to be. So. "I can't say."

Her disappointment was quick, and she shrugged. "I hope she's okay. The others were saying her parents were worried."

"Most parents would be worried." Not his.

She took his statement to mean hers. "Right. I should go talk to them."

He didn't want to let her go. "Yes. I'll be waiting to hear how it went."

Again, she studied him, like she was trying to piece together why he was shoving her away but still being extremely supportive, even though they'd planned to lose themselves in each other for days.

He'd even asked permission to have her to himself, dammit.

"Okay," she finally said. "What if it doesn't work out? Then what?"

"We can go to Earth and get a room." Her wings drooped like he'd let her down. Did she want to go to his place? "I still spend many nights in the barracks." Two buildings down from hers. "My house isn't comfortable. It just...is."

"It's not a home?"

He shook his head. If she stepped inside, then he'd get dangerous ideas. Thoughts that would destroy him more than an archmaster with a vial of angel fire. "No place is home for me."

~

Sitting in the sprawling main living room where Persephone used to sit with nothing to do while she was healing was like being transported to another time. The house had been more like a prison then. No. A cell. A dark corner where useless objects were set.

The same feelings were washing through her like she was on a rinse cycle. It didn't help that she felt like Urban had done everything but dump her out of the sky and onto the doorstep—anything that'd keep her away from his place.

Wasn't it weird that they'd planned three days together but not at his place? That they would've had to go to Earth to stay? Maybe that was the warrior way.

The single-warrior way. She inhaled steadily. Now wasn't the time to figure Urban out.

Her parents faced her, and judging by the disapproving looks on their faces when they answered the door, it was amazing she'd gotten this far.

Mother folded her arms and looked down her nose. "So now you want a place to stay?"

"I don't need one if that's what you're suggesting. I could stay in the barracks." Persephone ignored the pinch to her heart. If she hadn't wanted to repair things with her parents, was that where she would've ended up?

Was that where she'd end up regardless? She wasn't sure whether Mother had cut her off or if they could have a solid mother-daughter relationship. An ache settled into her chest. She'd like that.

She'd grown up so much while she was gone—all of it necessary. Were they ready to notice? "I have three days off before my next phase of training, and I thought maybe we could talk or something. Since you two still have to work, I could stay if that'd be easier."

"'Talk or something.'" Her mother tsk-tsked. "You had plenty of time to talk to us."

"Not when you'd listen."

Mother drew back, and Father put his head down. His beard had grown bushier since she'd left. She'd like to think it was from worry, but perhaps he no longer felt the need to make up for his daughter's lack by keeping his hair in place.

Persephone spread her hands. "Look, I'd like to have an actual parent-kid thing with you two, but I'm also not going to tolerate being made to feel less than, like I'm not enough—smart enough, savvy enough, ambitious enough."

"Actions speak louder than—"

"Can anyone here argue my recent actions?" She'd never interrupted her mother so much in her life. "Anyone? You never made it a secret you'd rather I was more like the Montclaire sisters. That I was a disappointment. I'm interested in serving the realm. I'm actively training for it. Fairly, even. But I'm learning to be the Persephone I should've been years ago. And if you can't accept the grown-up version of her, then I'll leave and we won't talk again."

How she kept her voice strong, she didn't know. She was tempted to return to the little girl hiding in her room and crying because her mother had admonished her yet again for telling a joke when there were More Serious Things to worry about.

Persephone had been through More Serious Things. She needed jokes more than ever.

Her mother lifted her chin. "You certainly are different from how you were."

"I was what I felt was expected of me when I couldn't be the daughter you wanted."

Moisture glittered in Mother's eyes. "Oh, Persephone. I

never meant to make you feel that way. It's just that…" She blew out a hard breath, and her wings curled around herself. "You can only see so many people get their wings cut off and hear the atrocities of the demons before you carry the burden home and dump it out for everyone to suffer."

Father rubbed Mother's back. His cautiously hopeful gaze was on Persephone. "If I had my way, you'd stay with us and never leave. There's peace in knowing you're safe." His smile was sad. "Safe and miserable is another story. I don't want that. I think I can speak for both me and your mother when I say we'd at least like to have an open-door policy with you. That this house will always welcome you, in whatever iteration you choose."

Unexpected tears welled in Persephone's eyes. "I'd like that." She had a job to do, but she wanted her parents to be part of her life. She swiped at a hot tear rolling down her cheek. "Do you, uh, know what type of shoes a lazy person wears?"

Her mother huffed out a laugh and buried her face in her hands. "I can't believe I actually missed those stupid jokes."

Father put his finger up. "Let me think." He blinked at the ceiling. "I don't know. Numen don't wear much for shoes, but I certainly know some lazy angels."

More laughter sputtered out of Mother. "Oh, dear, don't I know it."

Persephone grinned. "Loafers."

Mother sighed, but her smile remained in place. "I missed you. I really did." Persephone didn't know what to say, and Mother continued. "I was so worried about you, and then you went to training, and I now know what real worry is. Are you sure you want to be a warrior? Did I drive you away? Is it revenge?"

"It's not revenge," Persephone said softly. "I know what real pain is. And if I can prevent it for anyone else, I'll make it my mission to do so."

Mother's gaze danced over her. "Yes, I do believe you will. And I couldn't be prouder. Your room is all ready for you."

"Speaking of that, there's one more thing I'd like to talk to you about."

CHAPTER 13

Urban stared at the second-story window. He was back to stealing into her room. Full circle almost. They weren't exactly sneaking around, admitting to no one they had a friendship, much less a romantic relationship. Before, he'd never cared who knew what about him. He preferred his dating life to be discreet—and dating had been a strong word. He'd fucked around, sometimes with the same person, sometimes not.

But standing on the grass and gazing at those wide-open French doors, he wished he could stride through the front door and pick her up in his arms. Which was exactly what he didn't want. He didn't need a relationship to flaunt around the realm, and speculation was the last thing she needed. Her accomplishments were her own, not because she was fucking him.

But he wanted her to be fucking him. Except she was in her bedroom again, and there'd be none of that. She wasn't injured, and this time he was here because he couldn't resist her.

Finally, when the lights had been out in the lower level

for a while and he sensed no movement from inside, he quietly flew to Persephone's balcony. He carefully closed the doors as he entered.

Unlike when he'd done this before, she was sitting up in bed. Instead of an open-back gown, she wore a normal nightshirt that fit around her wings, and her long legs were tucked under her blankets.

"Hey," she whispered. "What do you call a guy lying in front of a door?"

His lips twitched and some of the self-imposed tension drained out of him. "Matt."

Her smile was shadowed, but he'd missed seeing her like this. He liked her no matter where she was or how she was dressed, but the casual Persephone, comfortable in her own skin, was a treat he wanted to indulge in for the rest of his life.

His steps faltered, and she straightened like she was worried he'd fall and make a racket. He reached the bed and crawled on top of the covers, trying to keep his mind off the thought that had flittered through a few seconds ago.

Rest of his life.

He wanted her. Forever.

For a guy who didn't do commitment, he'd mentally flung around forever with no warning.

"How'd it go?" he asked. Her relationship with her parents was paramount. Forever wasn't for them.

"Good. Really well, actually." She dropped her gaze to her clasped hands. It was as if she was afraid to touch him, like he was hesitant to put his hands on her—he'd never stop. "Mother said she was proud of me."

"She should be."

She fiddled with her fingers. "They said you could come for supper tomorrow night."

"Are you asking me on a date?" He sounded like he was joking, but the emotions roiling inside him were nothing like when they shared jokes.

"It was kind of a preplanned date, but yes. Officially, would you like to come over for a meal tomorrow? Meet my parents?" She injected a teasing tone.

"What'd you tell them?"

"That we got to know each other after you helped save me, but we wanted to wait until I was further along in training."

They hadn't made it that far.

"That's good." He scooted closer until he reclined alongside her. His face was close to her breasts, which moved evenly with her breathing, unbound and ripe for the picking.

Perhaps it was the fear from when he used to sneak in, but he couldn't bring himself to make a move on her with her parents in the same house. It might be different if they knew he was there. Weird but different. Less wrong.

She wiggled under the covers until their faces were aligned. "Aren't you going to join me?"

It'd be so easy. They could be quiet, and he'd be inside her in minutes. He wouldn't even have to take his pants off. But his warrior honor remained solid. "I can't." His voice came out strangled. "Your parents. It just seems wrong."

She was quiet, then she tried to stifle a snicker.

"What?" He didn't think ignoring his massive erection was a laughing matter.

"I always thought you were hot because you were, like, a bad boy, even though you're a warrior. But you won't do anything until you get approval and meet my parents properly."

"I've done a lot to you, or have you forgotten?"

Her laughter dried up and the same level of need

reflected in her eyes. "I haven't forgotten. I think it's really honorable that you won't touch me. I like it."

He pressed a light kiss to her hair. That was as far as he'd go. "I should leave, then."

"Well… You don't have to touch me, but I can touch myself."

His brain spun to register what she said, but his dick got the message loud and clear. His heartbeat reverberated through his erection until he wished his pants would evaporate. He'd fly home wearing nothing but his shoes and a shirt just to get some relief. "What?"

Oh, he'd heard—every syllable.

She slipped a hand under the covers, and he raptly watched the mound her arm made under the bedding, closer to where he wished he could taste.

"Persephone." His whisper was ragged.

"Urban," she countered, and the bed shifted as she widened her legs.

She was really going to do it. He should go, but he couldn't find one damn reason why his ass should leave the bed.

Pushing the covers down, she arched. Her hard nipples were obvious through the fabric of her nightshirt. She cupped a hand over her breast, and a low moan left her.

"You're going to kill me." He could barely whisper. All his energy was being used to hold himself still so he wouldn't slam himself on top of her and drive away.

"Urban, I'm wet."

He squeezed his eyes shut. "I know just how you'd taste. Are you circling your clit like I'd do with my tongue?"

"Exactly like." The words were breathless. The bedding shifted again as she started rocking her hips with her strokes. "I can feel you inside me."

It was his turn to groan. "Fuck, Persephone. Tell me more."

She tweaked her nipple with her thumb, and his gaze narrowed on her tit like he was a bird of prey. "I want your mouth right here." She tapped her breast a moment before pulling down the collar. A dark dusky bead was bared, and his mouth watered.

Just a little tongue?

No. He held firm, a tremble rocking his body. She liked that he was being honorable, so he'd be goddamn honorable if it killed him.

She cut off a groan. "I'm going to be loud."

"Don't be. This is just for us."

She whimpered and bit her lip. Her teeth dug in to what had to be a point of pain. Fuck, he couldn't let her hurt when she was only supposed to experience pleasure.

He caught her lips. She greedily opened for him and sucked on his tongue. The bed's slight shaking increased until she arched. Her ass left the mattress. She was coming. He kept his hands to himself. His cock was throbbing, but he'd done it. When she sank into the bedding, he pulled away and licked his lips.

A sigh left her. "Not as good as you."

"Soon."

She used the hand that had been on her breast to caress his face. "Soon. It's going to be hard pretending that you were never here when I go down for breakfast. Mother and Father will be there. They like to wake up and complain about everyone they work with."

What would that be like? Wake up to Persephone, sit at the table, and shit talk annoying warriors. Bitch about senate politics, and then he'd take her on the table before they left for work.

Something that had seemed like a living nightmare

before hit differently now that he was back in bed with her, chatting, while the sounds of her orgasm still reverberated in his ears.

But she was still in training, and he couldn't buy the idea of domestic bliss. So…it was nothing but a daydream.

THE HUM in her body the next morning wasn't as strong as when Urban had gotten her off. Persephone was already out of bed and lightly toeing downstairs. It wasn't that she was trying to sneak up on her parents; she wanted to test her stealth. A barracks full of warriors could either be noisy or eerily quiet, depending on how training had gone. In a couple of days, she'd be on Earth, stalking demons and possessed hosts.

Her parents would be surprised she was up so early. When she was recovering, it'd taken forever to talk herself into the agony of getting out of bed. Before that, she'd slumber until almost lunchtime. Easier to miss the ambitious folks going off to work.

She was almost to the kitchen when she heard Mother say, "It's weird having her back."

Stopping, she bit her lip. It'd be polite to continue into the dining area. She didn't want to intrude, but…the old part of herself that had learned a lot from eavesdropping was stronger under this roof.

"Mm." A slurping noise. Father's main bad habit and one her mother had grown deaf to. "I have a hard time not seeing her as the little girl skulking around. But she's made it through half of warrior training."

"I got it out of Odessa that Persephone has already done some demon hunting. The director wanted to make sure she wouldn't panic and flunk out of training."

"You didn't get it out of Odessa." Worldly knowledge oozed from her father. "The director gave her permission to tell you so you wouldn't worry so much."

Persephone's lips twitched. Her father was likely right.

Mother chuckled. "They're a good pair. Good for the realm. Her sister too."

"And much of the senate respects him."

"Senator Thomas keeps asking what I think of him."

Senator Thomas was so old Persephone didn't think he was interested in much anymore. She envisioned him blowing the dust off himself every morning after being in a catatonic state most of the night. The guy was just ancient.

"He's grieving and looking for someone to blame," Father said.

"I urged him to talk to Bryant. To tell him about Tommy. Something just doesn't seem right."

"Darling, haven't you learned to stay far away from that? We're senators. We're not realm enforcers, and we're not warriors."

"No, but our daughter lives here. What if there's someone else like Juliette Colbert in the senate?" Mother hissed. "What if it's someone we don't dare question?"

Persephone's heart beat harder, and the ache in her back grew in strength. That vile female. *Please, child. Call me Juliette.*

"Senator Colbert was too entitled to act with others," Father said.

"I wish that was the case, but I wonder. The way she framed her mate. That's a lot for one female."

"She had the enforcers she'd recruited or paid off. The arrogance of senators is what gets them into trouble, but is also what makes it hard for them to plot treason."

"True." Mother paused. "I just think... We're done with that mess, yet I just wish..."

"What, darling?"

Another exhale. "I wish I didn't feel like I had to worry so much. Persephone's come so far, but she's still so young."

"But when we didn't worry, we were really just oblivious."

Mother chuckled. "True. I guess we'll just have to pray that our daughter has indeed trained and can no longer be targeted."

Persephone shook her wings. No more. Their thoughts about her were private, and she'd respect that. She needed to talk to them about having Urban over for a meal, but mostly, to start getting to know them.

CHAPTER 14

Ransom prowled through Elodie's house. The blinds were drawn, and the lights were off. She was supposed to be living alone. Ransom would sleep in her cramped office. He'd lie low and keep from being seen. To anyone watching, the house was empty while Elodie was away.

After discussing options with the director, they had a plan. And today, Elodie was to have stood outside the senate coliseum glaring at the entrance. It sounded absurd. It sounded too simple. It'd probably work, and the thought made his skin crawl.

The last several weeks, he'd been training with her. Talking with her. She knew about his family, making her one of the few people he could be himself with. He treasured her.

As fond as he was of her, he also felt…other things. Sensations and emotions he'd blocked out a long time ago —when Sierra's fate was put into his hands. But there was more. Not only was it a struggle to keep his gaze off her chest and not wonder how warm her skin was or what her breasts would feel like against his palms, he wanted to hold her as much as he wanted to drive himself into her body until they were both spent. Afterward, they'd lie together and talk—about everything.

Even before he'd become a father, he hadn't been a talker. He'd dated Numen females and slept with human women. He'd always been friendly, but he'd never been close to anyone.

The front door opened, and he wiped the thoughts away. They were for another time when he didn't have to be concerned about her safety. "How'd it go?"

Her wings weren't droopy, but her brow was furrowed. "Weird." She bent to unhook the ankle straps of her sandals, and he marveled at the familiarity of the move. She could come home daily, sigh, take her shoes off, and tell him about her day. Two people who'd been strangers not long ago.

He'd known who she was in the realm. Had kept himself aloof from thoughts about her other than she was the fruit vendor's pretty daughter. But seeing her in a simple knee-length robe tied around her waist and showing the delicate flare to her hips was a new experience. He couldn't get enough of her.

Drinking her in before she straightened, he struggled to recall her answer. "Oh?"

"Yeah." She sighed as she kicked her sandals all the way off and padded toward the kitchen. "I went there after I visited my parents in the market. So, I thought I'd be all glowering. Stand in the corner and stare. But everyone stopped to talk to me. Everyone."

"Why?"

She shrugged and moved to the counter. Instead of getting food, she lifted herself to perch on the edge. "It's like I'm suddenly popular. I think my parents talked about me so much at the market, how worried they were about me after Tommy's death, so they all were surprised to see me. Even Senator Thomas shuffled over and asked how I was doing." She made a disgusted noise. "Everyone was so nice. I tried to be sullen. What do they call that personality on Earth? Emo?"

"How awful," he said wryly but sobered when she only scowled. "I know it's frustrating, but that's actually a good sign. They might be legitimately friendly, or they might be testing out where you're at and what you know. They might be trying to gain your trust."

"I'll never trust any of them." She swung her legs, and the edges of her robe fell open.

His gaze was riveted. Inch by inch, her skin was revealed. He could see more of her inner thighs leading to darkness. If he stooped down, would he be able to see—

He yanked his gaze up and found her studying him. Guilty, he pushed a hand through his hair. "You're right not to trust them until they've proven trustworthy."

"I trust you," she murmured and slid off the counter and closed the distance between them. "Ransom?"

"Yeah?" he asked, his voice thick.

"I'm really glad you're here." She trailed her fingers over a bicep. He was wearing his typical warrior garb, and he wished the sleeves were short, so she could touch his skin. "I didn't like the idea of coming back to an empty house."

"Because you're scared of being attacked?"

She picked an invisible fleck of lint off his sleeve. "Yes." Another sigh left her. "Ugh. No." She jerked her hand away and stomped toward the living room.

He followed. "Elodie?"

She spun, and the hem of her robe swirled up. He couldn't stop himself from looking.

She stabbed a finger toward him. "That."

"What?"

"You." She crossed to him, and he didn't move, relishing how close they were. "Is it me, or have we been doing this will-they-or-won't-they dance for weeks? Will you kiss me? Do you even like me? What if I make a move and it gets rebuffed? It'd be humiliating."

"I do like you. A lot. And I want to kiss you." When her lips parted, he couldn't resist. He cupped her chin, swiping his thumb across her bottom lip. "So very much."

"Why don't you?"

"I was afraid of the same. And how you'd accept the important people in my life." She was one of the important people too. "Now we're in a bigger situation. I can't distract us with my attraction. And...I wasn't sure how you felt."

"Do I need to spell it out?"

That was close enough. He dipped his head and set his lips on hers. A simple touch but a big move for them both. For weeks, they'd been separated by a chasm full of doubts and fears. But he'd seen this female with his grandson. She was helping his team keep not only his family but the entire realm safe.

She gripped his arms, and he deepened the kiss. When she opened for him, he groaned. So sweet. The tangle of her tongue with his. The way she held on to him like he was her anchor. She had wound her way into his life, and he didn't know whether he could go back to his empty house. Maybe when all this was over—

He pulled back. The haziness in her gaze almost had him leaning forward again and continuing where they had left off, but he straightened. "This isn't over." A phrase with a few meanings. "You and me? We're picking up where we left off, but I can't be caught with my hand down your pants if someone breaks in."

The flare of desire in her eyes made him all too aware he had an erection protesting its neglect. "I understand."

"The mission isn't done either. Once that's over"—he stroked his fingers down her face again because he needed to touch her—"then you and I can pick up where we left off."

"I'd like that."

He wanted to rejoice, but there was one thing he had to make sure was straight between them. "About Sierra and—"

This time, she placed her finger on his lips. "I'm dedicated to getting the word out, but also…I get it. I really do. I want to tell the truth, to inform the realm, but I want to keep the innocents safe."

Sierra wasn't innocent. Arik was. Boone. But that was a complication for another day.

PERSEPHONE RACED to the front door of her parents' place and flung it open. A nervous Urban stood on the other side. His wings rose, then dropped like he was afraid the movement would come off as aggression. He had a fruit basket in one hand. Then he switched it to the other.

"Come in." Her nerves were fired up. When she'd told her parents he was coming over, they'd gotten worked up all over again.

Wasn't he involved in your training? How inappropriate is that? What—exactly—did you two do in the human realm?

She'd been firm that she and Urban would talk to them tonight.

He stepped in, and his leather-and-soap scent wafted over her. She was used to smelling him on her sheets, on her skin, but getting to enjoy it in an open part of her house meant they were making progress. Meant they were an item.

His gaze lifted over her shoulder, and he swallowed. "Senator Nassim." He nodded. "Senator Nassim."

When she turned, both her parents were glowering at him.

"We trusted her with you and the director." Mother's tone was cold enough to crack the marble floor.

Well, that wasn't progress.

"Mother." Persephone hooked an arm through Urban's. "You didn't have a choice. I was training whether you trusted them or not, remember?"

Father's eyebrow twitched. "Come. Sit. We might as well get it all out before we eat. I don't want to be tense with my food."

Once they were stiffly sitting—Mother and Father on the couch, Urban on a backless cushioned stool, and Persephone on the edge of a settee, farther from Urban than she wanted—Mother was the first to speak.

"I don't like how this started between you two."

"First of all," Persephone said, "you don't know how it started. That's part of what we want to discuss. Urban helped save me with Bronx and Tosca, you know that." They nodded, not looking any happier. "Well, he tried to visit, and you ran him off."

Mother's gaze flicked to Urban, no guilt visible in her expression. She turned her attention back to Persephone. "You needed rest."

"I also needed support." Persephone glanced at Urban. His profile was stoic, and tension radiated from his wide shoulders. "I needed to feel like myself."

"I visited her," Urban said. "Every night I could."

"You broke into our house?" Father sputtered.

"No. He was invited in." After he'd broken in the first

time. She kept her tone gentle. There was enough animosity in the room. "By me. I lived here too, and like I said, I needed more than I was getting from you."

"We didn't do anything," Urban said in a rush. "We told jokes and talked." He stared at his hands and a shadow crossed his face. "I first came out of guilt—and concern. But I realized she wasn't anything like I'd thought, and then I just really enjoyed visiting her. It was nothing more than that for a long time. I promise."

Father gazed at him for a moment. "You're an honorable male, Urban, but we know your reputation. You'd have us believe you were in our daughter's room every night and nothing happened?"

Irritation flashed hot in her chest. "And so what if it did? I'm an adult. This is my home too. I am an adult, even if I didn't act like it for years."

"Persephone…" Mother did that senator thing. The *we can all be reasonable* tone.

"No. Either I'm an adult, or I'm not. You believe us, or you don't. Either way, I'm seeing Urban. Tonight is just for you to decide whether you want to be upset or have a good time."

Mother drew herself straighter. She might have been sitting, but her wings were high and proud. "I'd like to enjoy my time with my daughter, and I don't want to see her heart get broken when Urban does what he does best. No offense." She smiled like she didn't care if anyone was offended—because she didn't. "I respect you, but I also know how you are. And your parents."

Persephone gasped.

Urban cleared his throat. "I'd prefer you keep them out of this."

"Have you brought Persephone to meet them?"

His jaw clenched. "We're not close."

"You're not close to anyone, it seems," Mother said.

"Enough." Persephone rose. She held her hand out to Urban, but his bleak expression didn't look promising. She clenched her fingers into a fist and put her other hand over it. Why was she attempting to earn respect when her parents weren't cooperating? "It seems my welcome has been worn out. I'll grab my things."

Mother and Father rose as a unit.

Mother took a step toward her. "You're leaving over him?"

"I'm leaving over your treatment of him."

Urban's head was bowed, but he rose. "My apologies." He walked toward the door, and Persephone followed him out. When she closed the door behind her, about to tell him to wait while she grabbed her things, he faced her on the stoop. "They're right, you know."

"About what? You're not worried about me being in training, are you? I thought we were past that point."

"I'm not close to anyone. I never was."

"Weren't you and Bronx inseparable before he and Tosca mated?"

His right eye twitched as if he didn't like being reminded Bronx's life had changed and he was no longer a constant part of it. "I'm not interested in mating. I was honest with you up front."

"Well, that makes this so much better." She gave a weary sigh. She was tired of the constant push and pull. Did he or didn't he? Her parents. The years of tugging against her true self and stuffing that girl into a box. She pinched the bridge of her nose. "We only just revealed our relationship to my parents. You don't talk to yours. The director might know about us, but not your team. We aren't at eternity level yet, Urban. We're in a can-we-or-can't-we period."

They could be something special. She thought they

already were. Her feelings were strong. Genuine. But then, it wasn't up to her.

"I know," he said, "but before we get too far along, perhaps it's best to pull back. You just reconciled with your parents, and I'm a setback." His worried gaze pierced the door. "I don't want to come between you and them. The rift between you has only just been closed. It hasn't even been sealed shut. My presence is ripping it open like a gaping wound."

"Their attitude is. Letting me stay under the same roof isn't the same as accepting me. What they did in there was the same thing they've been doing for years."

Urban's wings hung low. Defeat was written over his face. "Persephone. Stay here. Let them get to know the wonderful warrior you're becoming. They'll be there for you far longer than I will be."

She drew back. "You're giving up before we even start?"

"I'm saying that eternity is a long time."

She had a decision to make. Beg or accept. There was a third option—negotiate. Begging was a temptation she couldn't dwell on. She hadn't progressed this far to beg a man she'd already had to confront about his feelings, likewise, with negotiation. She could barter for time, to wait until her month of field training was done. But no. She'd come too far to be that female.

She'd accepted herself. He needed to work on his reality. She couldn't help him. "Okay."

His dark brows pulled together. "Okay?" His tone asked, *just like that?*

Yes. Just like that. She put her hand on the large golden door handle. "I respect your feelings. I wish we could've been more."

"Persephone."

She waited, hoping he'd tell her he was sorry, that he

was mistaken and wanted her to come to his empty house and fill it with love. Because she did love him. She'd loved him since he first walked into her room and listened to a joke.

"I'm sorry, Percy."

The nickname made his decision even worse. "Me too."

CHAPTER 15

Urban stabbed the toe of his boot into the dirt. Evergreens towered over him. A week had passed since he'd told Persephone it was best they didn't continue their relationship. Sierra and Boone's place had become the waiting ground as if the team was afraid of becoming embroiled in another conflict before the current mission was over. The backyard was bigger than most counties, and he spent his time wandering in the fresh air, trying to clear the cloud of doubts from his head.

"What'd that rock do to you?" Bronx joked.

Urban scowled at him. He and Bronx had been inseparable. The rest of their team had slowly paired off, and he and Bronx had done what they did best—fuck around on their time off. But Bronx was constantly going back to Numen to be with his mate. And when he was around, he was focused on the mission. He was no longer the fuck-around type.

Urban wasn't either. Perhaps one day he'd go back to his bachelor ways.

Just the thought made his gut churn, his body ready to evict his innards with the very idea.

Yeah. He was fucked.

"Seriously, Urban. What's going on?"

If it weren't for the concern in Bronx's tone, Urban might not have answered. "Persephone and I have a thing. Had a thing."

Bronx's surprise registered in his lifted brows. He crossed his arms. "The same Persephone we rescued in Florida?"

"She's not the same." He dug his boot into a partially buried rock. "Not anymore."

"I heard. She's almost done with her warrior basics and then she'll be an intern for a year. That's pretty impressive—for a senator's kid, for what happened to her, and for…"

"How she used to act?"

"She was a little heinous."

Urban nodded. "We don't wear each other's brand, so it's not like it was going to work."

"Sync mates are more complicated than that."

He shrugged. Didn't matter. "I know how mating works."

"Don't your parents have some sort of messed-up—"

"Yes." Urban wandered a few more steps. He should've brought Boone's fishing equipment and caught something for dinner. Then he'd feel useful. All this time spent waiting only kept thoughts swirling in his head. "They hate each other."

"Wasn't your father a warrior?"

"Yep."

Bronx snapped his fingers. "And he got injured. Your mother got a sync brand and saved him."

"Sure did."

"And now you think that because they don't like each other, mating is a scheme and not for you?"

"Fuck, Bronx." He rolled his shoulder. For a guy used to long-term morphs, his back was tight. "There's the director."

"What about him?"

"You weren't there. After his injuries, his first sync mate saw him and panicked and got herself killed." The couple that was Director Vale and Odessa had formed as an agreement when the director had been their team leader. He'd been ordered to take a mate since his first one had fled from him and his injuries. Odessa had accepted his mating request because she'd been scared for her life. They loved each other now. They were wild about each other. How long would that last?

"Wasn't he a pretty gruesome sight?" Bronx asked.

Half the director's face smoldering with angel fire? Yes. The female had been young, naive, and Numen was a vain realm. Being sentenced to a disfigured male had likely terrified her. "Just think, though. She would've been miserable."

"Or they would've been deeply in love."

Irritation toward Bronx made Urban smack his lips. "What about Odessa?"

"If the director had gotten mated, then he and Odessa would've been inhabitants of the same realm and nothing more."

Urban ground his teeth together. He wandered down the path a little farther. Blue winked between the boughs of the trees. He regretted not bringing that fishing gear. If his mind wouldn't quit, he could at least have something to do with his hands.

Bronx stepped in front of him. "Listen. We don't have guarantees in life, not even us, with our healing and our long lives and our realm full of angels. I thought I'd be a bachelor until I was injured so badly I'd be assigned a mate. Then came Tosca. Sierra was a fucking fallen. Who thought she'd mate a *human*? And look at Sandeen and Harlowe? That one's not on a bingo card."

"Eternity is a long time."

"Sure is. And I'm grateful I get to argue and make up with Tosca for centuries." He waggled his brows. "It's the making up that's—"

"Don't you fucking finish that sentence." The taste and feel of Persephone haunted him. What she'd done to herself while he watched was a ready show every time he closed his eyes. Then he'd fucked up the next night.

Eternity was a long time to go without experiencing her again.

He glowered at the rocky path. "All of our team's relationships are new."

"My parents' isn't. Persephone's parents. Our old director, Leo Richter; when humans talk about 'in sickness and in health,' I think Leo and Millie Richter encompass that."

It was on the tip of his tongue to claim those relationships weren't the same, but he couldn't figure out why.

"Hell, Urban. Dionna wasn't on a long personal hiatus because she and her mate were on a belated honeymoon. They had some serious shit to work through. But they did it, and when I joked about making up, I was actually quite serious. Learning to fight and make up and communicate is as critical as chemistry. More important than some mark on our wrist. And I don't know your mother and father, but I wonder how much they tried."

"They didn't care enough to."

"There you go. Yet they're what you're basing your decision on."

"What if I've fucked up?"

Bronx let out a lengthy sigh. "What did I just say? About making up?"

Right. If Urban couldn't figure out that much, did he really have any business in a relationship?

Training was going well, and it was nice to be doing something more worthwhile than sparring, which Persephone was in the middle of now. She followed the young woman to the restroom. The human appeared to be close in age to Persephone. When the woman banged into the restroom, Persephone slipped inside. Kadee was at the sink.

Kadee spun and the woman stiffened, thanks to the demon using her as a host. It recognized what Kadee was.

"She knows," Persephone said. The rest of the room was empty. She slapped her hand on the woman's shoulder, spoke the incantation, and Kadee dove to transcend to the Mist with her.

By the time cool droplets dotted her face, Persephone had her dagger drawn. The archmaster that had possessed the woman faced her. A yawning mouth that either had never had a lower jaw or had lost it in a fight dripped pus-filled saliva.

Persephone's stomach had been lined with steel for the last two weeks. Stana had scoped out several high-risk humans since they'd been on Earth, and the training team was working overtime dispatching demons.

The creature lunged for her while striking. A claw might've raked her face if Kadee hadn't grabbed the demon's wings and yanked it backward. Persephone ducked closer and stabbed her knife into the creature's abdomen. A shrill screech scraped her eardrums.

The demon yanked itself free from Kadee's hold. Just as it was about to leap on Persephone, Kadee dumped her vial of angel fire on it.

Persephone skittered back. She was used to handling angel fire now, thanks to Urban, but she was still cautious.

After the demon shriveled into ashy remains, Persephone faced Kadee.

"Another one down." Her friend's grin was triumphant.

Persephone's smile lagged. "Good job, partner."

Kadee nodded. "Too bad Molly couldn't get to us in time." Molly had been farther behind Persephone. Kadee propped her hands on her hips. "While we're in private, why have you been such a downer?"

"I've been fine."

Kadee tipped her head. "Don't think I haven't noticed a certain growly warrior hasn't been hanging around."

She hadn't heard from him since he'd left her parents' place two weeks ago. "We're training in the field."

"That didn't matter when we were working by the barracks. He'd come by all the time."

"Now he doesn't." Why was she being evasive? Kadee was her friend, and if she'd noticed Persephone's behavior, then Persephone wanted to make sure she wasn't messing up. "Fine. We broke up."

Kadee's eyes widened. "You two were a real thing?"

"No. Breakup's a strong word. He gave up just as we were going to try to be a thing."

"Why?"

Persephone wiped her shoes on the damp grass. She'd worn her boots, but to blend with the humans, she had put jeans on. Guys could get away with looking like security better than a girl with a big bust and wide hips could. Kadee was dressed in her warrior gear but with a cool beanie as if she cosplayed as an urban street fighter every day.

What should she say? It wasn't Kadee's business. But it was Persephone's, and she had a friend for once. One she trusted with her life. Perhaps she could confide in her too. "He has baggage about relationships and how they don't work for eternity."

Kadee snorted. "I get that."

"You do?"

"Oh, yeah." She stooped to clean off her dagger. She must've gotten some slices in before breaking out the angel fire. "My mother and father have an open relationship, and for a long time, it messed with my head. None of my parents' friends did."

"So you're fine with it now?"

"I'm not sure I'd ever get used to open personally. To each their own, but they're my parents, and you know how we're raised—eternity. One mate. Like we're not sure if it's a bad thing or good thing. But then I realized my parents aren't open per se. They're roommates. They even have separate bedrooms."

"Oh."

"Yeah. But they don't argue like they did when I was younger. And who knows, maybe in a century they'll decide to try monogamy again."

Bile rose in Persephone's throat. She didn't like the idea of sporadic monogamy for herself. Not with Urban.

Maybe it was for the best he put a stop to them.

"I don't know why they even mated," Kadee continued. "I think they were afraid to get hurt while fighting and who they'd get paired with."

"Fate's not supposed to give us a bad mate."

"No, but we're still Numen. Stubborn, set in our ways, and think we're above silly emotions."

Persephone's chuckle was soft, but she was thinking about how Urban's parents must've affected him.

Should she have negotiated? Told him to wait until training was done and then they'd take it slow? She wouldn't want him to doubt her or them. "There's nothing I can do about it now. Even when I go into probation status, I'm going to be tied up with work."

"Yeah, but we'll get time off. If you two are meant to be, it'll happen."

"Wouldn't it be happening right now?"

Kadee's shrug was nonchalant. "Perhaps fate was working and you two are getting in the way. It'll work out. We should get back to the safe house and clean up. I'll notify Mac and Molly if you take care of the report to Stana."

"Yeah, no problem." She could bang out a description of the fight while her mind was tangled in thoughts of fate and Urban. She could do her duty while wondering whether fate could fix what she and Urban might've broken.

CHAPTER 16

Three weeks of living under the same roof as Elodie had been a mixture of heaven and hell. He wanted to kiss her again—to devour her. But he had to be on alert. And he was restless. So damn bored he was about to shoot through the roof and do barrel rolls in the sky.

He paced, sick of the dim rooms. His home was open, with wide windows. He'd wanted Sierra's life to be bright and optimistic after hers had begun in terrible darkness. But because of the need for concealment, Elodie's drapes were open only when she was home, and that was only for short amounts of time so she could report to him about her days. She made sure to furtively glance outside for anyone monitoring her when she opened and closed the window treatments.

When the sun streamed in, he stayed hidden in her office. She'd make supper and bring him food. Often she sat with him while he ate, his favorite part of the day.

The front door cracked open, and her voice drifted in

louder than usual. "Thank you for checking on me. I really appreciate it. It's been so hard without Tommy."

Ransom darted for the office and dove inside. Then he spun and crouched by the door, out of sight from whoever entered but ready to interfere if someone was trying to hurt her.

An old, familiar voice drifted in. Senator Thomas. "I'm glad, dear. Tommy's death was a shock to all of us and a blow to the realm. I know you were closer to him than anyone. I've been worried about you."

"Thanks for checking in. Want to, uh, come in?"

Ransom tensed. He could remain hidden. The senator was an elder, so perhaps his senses weren't as sharp as they'd been five hundred years ago. But Ransom didn't want to risk it. He could explain his presence as Elodie's lover and that she was worried people would think she was moving on too quickly, but it wouldn't explain her behavior over the last few weeks. Anyone after her would stay far away from her house.

"No, no," the senator said. "I hate to bother you. I'm sure a young female like you has plenty of plans for the evening."

"No, it's just me. Without Tommy…" She left it hanging. Smart. Finishing it might leave the tinge of a lie on the air.

"I understand. I can give you some enforcers' names if you ever need help. I know your parents are close."

"I don't talk to them a lot."

"Yes, well, stay strong, dear. You were important to Tommy, and I'd hate to have anything happen to you."

"Thank you, Senator." The front door clicked shut, but Ransom stayed where he was. Better safe than sorry. Senator Thomas was a constant of the realm, but perhaps that was why he'd been overlooked.

The blinds swished as Elodie opened them. She sat on

the couch closest to the hallway nook that hid the office entry. Her voice floated in, aimed at him. "That was…nice?"

Ransom squatted by the doorframe where he could see her. "Did you sense a lie when he departed?"

Her profile was contemplative. He drank her in. Strong nose. Glossy black hair. Dusky wings that he wanted to sink his fingers into as he bent her over—

He cleared his throat.

"Sorry," she said. "I was trying to figure out what I felt."

"No. No rush." Just him being a pervert.

"No different than being around him usually. I always got an odd feeling around him when Tommy and I would visit. He's just…different."

"Age?"

"Maybe." She pushed off the couch and walked into the office, then shut the door behind her and slid down the wooden panel. "It's been weeks, Ransom."

"You lured the senator here."

"What if he was legitimately checking on me? What if the real culprit knows we're onto him? What if…" She sighed and propped her head in her hands, her elbows on her knees. "What if we're wasting time?"

"We're Numen; we have plenty of time."

She peered at him through her arms. "Tommy didn't. I wasted six months of his life when I wasn't really into him. He could've found someone. He could've known what it was like to be madly in lust with someone."

"Not madly in love?"

"What I've been suffering through is lust," she mumbled.

His world came to a stop. "What are you really saying, El?"

She lifted her head. "I like when you call me El."

He'd only just started. "It makes me feel closer to you when we can't, you know, do anything else."

"Oh, I know. Why again?"

"There might be an intruder while I'm buried deep inside you."

She peered at him over her shoulder. "How deep?"

"El, you're killing me."

She got up and crossed to him, kneeling in front of him. "Can I just be really quiet?"

He shouldn't have been considering her suggestion. But she was so close. The energy between them crackled. If the source of the constant treason in the realm was Senator Thomas, he'd be too clever to attack tonight. If the source wasn't him, well, then the house could be infiltrated in moments or never.

And then what? He sat on the floor and drew her toward him. "I can be quiet too. Just once? To get it out of our system so we can concentrate better?"

"Once."

Even as she said it and her lips descended on his and she pushed him back and crawled over him, he knew once would never be enough. He was a male who'd take what he could get from a female for whom he was spiraling out of control.

Between them, they got her robe off and his shirt, then he shoved his pants down to his knees. He had to stay partially prepared…

Then she was poised over him, her back bowed so she could capture his lips. He could let her slam onto him and ride them both into oblivion, but in the bedroom, he was a lover, not a fighter. He tried to be as generous as he would be serving dessert to his date. Just because they were having a frantic quickie on her office floor didn't mean it couldn't be mind-blowing.

"Just wait," he whispered and captured her mouth again.

He trailed his fingers down her side, loving how she shivered against him, her hard nipples rubbing gently against his chest.

"The next time we do this, I'm taking my time." He skimmed his hand along her belly and slipped between her legs. Her eyes went hazy, and she let out a low moan.

"Sorry." She didn't sound sorry.

"I'm only sorry I can't hear those sweet sounds coming from you. I've been dying to know if you wanted this as much as me." He circled a finger around her clit. The back of his wrist was stroking his dick, and when she moved, it created delectable friction. He had to force his attention away, or he'd blow before he got inside her.

"Yes," she groaned, rocking against him. The gentle scrape of her breasts was a sensation he'd carry with him forever.

She ground into him, and when she was at her peak, she adjusted her hips to place him at her entrance. He thrust up. Her body gripped him as he slid in, her walls squeezing him as she bit her lip through her orgasm, her body shaking.

He kept his thrusts going, but his touch was light on her clit. She was shuddering, her hands pressed into his chest. Her wings arched away from her body, the feathers brushing against the office chair and the cot he'd been using.

"Ransom," she said on a low moan.

"Ride it right into another one." He had a mental blueprint for her body and knew exactly what she needed.

Her release coated his fingers. "I think I'm going to come again," she gasped.

He'd make sure of it. His climax pounded at the base of

his spine, waiting to be released, to race over the peak and catapult him into the stars. Just a little longer. He didn't know when they'd do this again, and the fact that she'd made herself a target was something he couldn't forget day in, day out.

She rode him right into another climax, and this time, he let himself explode with her, arching, his wing joints digging into the floor, helping to hold him up.

When she collapsed on top of him, he cradled her, running his hand over her back. They stayed connected; he wasn't ready to break apart. Just a couple minutes. Moments he'd treasure forever.

She made circles on one of his biceps. "I wish you could come to bed with me."

"Me too. But we haven't eaten yet. I put a pasta-and-chicken dish together; all you have to do is throw it in."

The circles continued. "You're a good guy."

"I try to be."

"Anyone would be lucky to have you."

"Would you… Would you feel lucky to have me?"

She lifted her head to meet his gaze. "What are you asking?"

"I don't know. We've been together for months, but suddenly, I feel like I'm rushing."

She swallowed and looked at the wall for a moment. "I feel the same. But I haven't gotten a sync brand."

"A lot of couples don't. They don't need them." He continued stroking his hand up and down her back. "I lived in fear of getting one for so long."

"You'd have to expose your daughter."

"When she was grown and gone, I thought I'd cursed myself."

"I didn't think I deserved anyone for leading Tommy on."

"I don't know if I deserve you, but I want you."

She dropped a kiss on his lips, and his cock twitched. He hadn't softened much, and more blood rushed into him. "Are you ready again?"

"It's been a long time, and you're very beautiful."

A pink tint crested her cheeks. She was blushing while she was naked and impaled by him. So sexy. "No one's said that to me before."

"It's true."

She kissed him again and rocked her hips. "We weren't technically done yet, right?"

Their one time wasn't officially over while he still had an erection. "No."

PERSEPHONE WAS THE LOOKOUT AGAIN. They'd taken turns at different points of the day. The last three weeks had been intense. Barely any sleep, constant hunting and fighting, regrouping, and venturing out again.

They were in Vegas. During her probation year, she would travel the world; she couldn't wait. Learning to blend as a tourist, and then after enough years, she'd be able to pass for a local. A lot of warriors didn't bother. They could hunt without passing as residents.

She tapped her fingers on her thigh while she scrolled through her phone, looking at nothing but trying to fade into the woodwork at the food court.

"Hey," a deep voice said at the edge of her booth. The wrong timbre with a different type of growl, one that didn't do anything for her.

She glanced up, offering the same haughty expression she used to don as a mask every day. "I'm done with my trash if you want to take it."

Confusion ran through the man's handsome face, but he didn't get the hint. "Waiting for anyone?"

She turned her attention back to her phone. The guy was demon-free. Thus, she wasn't interested. "Yup."

"Well, he's late."

She glanced up again. "I'm not into guys."

His smile faltered for a moment, then returned with max wattage. "'Sokay. I can help you change your—" He grunted and stumbled to the side. "Hey!"

"Beat it." Urban slid into the booth across from her.

"Dude, what the fuck?"

Urban cut the man a withering glare. The human thought for a moment then shook his head and lurched away.

Urban's expression softened when he met her gaze. "Hi."

"Hi." She was so damn happy to see him that she almost forgot they'd parted like they had—and that she was training. "Not that I'm not glad to see you, but I'm working."

"I know, but we both know there's nothing going on."

"There's a symaster riding the shoulder of the short-order cook in the pizza place."

"Too public. Stana's going to have one of the team follow him after work, and you'll take the demon at the man's home."

"Did you talk to her?" She didn't care, but it was easier to talk about that than ask why he was across from her.

"No." His gaze flicked over her body. "How are you?"

"Fine." Missing him. "You?"

"Shitty. I messed up." He grabbed the obligatory sandwich wrapper that allowed her to sit in the food court booth as long as she needed to. "About my parents."

"You don't have to—"

"Yes, I do. Because being with you has made me rethink everything, and I was…wrong."

Hope rose in her chest. A dangerous emotion. "About what?"

"Us." He started folding the wrapper. First in half. And then in half again. "My father was critically injured as a warrior, and my mother got his mark. She found him and healed him, and they mated. But they didn't get along. I don't know if they wanted to or if they decided to match the other's shitty attitude, but I grew up hearing how awful mates are. That I needed to keep my options open, but the best option was none. Being single and free."

"I can see how that messed with your head."

"He kept putting himself in terrible situations. Mother would have to track him down and save him. Then she'd yell all night about the human soul she didn't escort to the light. Repeat."

"That's awful. Your father was doing it on purpose?"

"He never admitted it, but now he sits in an apartment in the human realm and gets as drunk as he can until he heals, and repeat."

Self-destructive behavior. "All because he had to get mated?"

"That's my guess. Then there's my mother and how she thought she gave up the guy who could've been her forever because of the brand. She'd tell me that being alone is better than seeing the person you're supposed to mate being synced with someone else. I thought of us. What if I get hurt and it's not you who comes for me?"

Irrational anger built inside her gut. No. No way. "What about having faith it would be me?"

His smile was brief. "What about if you got hurt even worse than last time and the person who gets your mark isn't me? I couldn't live with the thought. I grew up with a certain impression of mating and eternity. But I'm opening up to…something else. With you. I only want you."

"I only want you too, Urban. And we don't have to rush into anything. I have another week of field training. Then a year with an experienced unit. And after that, I'll probably get put with a permanent team." She shrugged. "I know Numen take their long lives for granted, and we're not guaranteed a long life, but we have time. I just want to spend it with you. And I really don't think you and I grew so close for someone else to wear our marks. Maybe that's where fate steps in—when we're being stubborn."

"Your parents—"

"Will have to deal. They're not used to being shocked. They're not used to me standing up for myself. And they aren't used to not getting their way when they make demands. I love them. They'll always be in my life, but if they can't accept us, it's not our problem."

Her eyes strayed to a couple walking by, and she tried to stay nonchalant. Two archmasters roaming Vegas in their hosts like they were going to catch a show and head to Red Rock Canyon later.

"Looks like you have work to do," Urban said.

"It's a given."

He slid out of the booth and came to her side. She tilted her face up, but he kissed her forehead. "Be safe."

"I'll have another three-day pass after next week."

The corner of his mouth lifted. "I'd like at least one of those days." He leaned closer. "But I'll take all three."

"They're yours."

He walked off, and as much as she wanted to watch him go, she kept her attention on the couple as she sent a message to her team.

One week. Then she'd have time to work things out with Urban.

CHAPTER 17

*R*ansom hung out in the office doorway. It'd been a week since the sex on the office floor. The whole get-it-out-of-our-system plan had been bullshit. He'd had a raging boner each night, and her wildflowers-in-rain scent was cemented in his pores. "You sure this is a good idea?"

Elodie was taking her third nightly walk, but the realm wasn't dark enough for him to dodge between buildings and hedges to keep an eye on her.

"I have my tracker." She patted her necklace.

Sierra had disguised the device as a piece of jewelry, which would likely be overlooked since so many warriors wore vials of angel fire around their necks.

"It's not enough," Ransom growled.

She shot him an understanding smile. "I know. I'd be lying if I said I don't feel exposed or vulnerable, but they either know you're here or they think I'd get away if they stormed my house."

Or they were on the wrong track and the last month had been a waste.

Except for that one night.

It'd been a risk to be together, but he couldn't regret it. Even if something had happened while he'd been buried inside her, he'd have been hard-pressed to come up with an ounce of remorse.

As long as she was okay. That was the clincher.

And now she was going out when shadows were falling over the realm. The plan was a sound one. If no one tried to abduct her in her home, then while she was alone in a dark realm, they might.

Except Ransom would be stuck in that damn house, not knowing whether she was fighting for her life.

Elodie finished putting on her shoes by the settee and moved over to him. She put her hands on his chest, and he grasped her forearms through her long-sleeved shirt. The first night she'd proposed the idea of an evening walk, she'd been ready to head out in her typical robe.

No fucking way.

She was too exposed as it was. She needed as much armor as she could wear without being obvious. Even if it was loose linen pants and a blousy top.

"I'm as prepared as can be." She curled her fingers into his shirt.

He sighed. He'd be worried no matter who was walking out that door, but he was beside himself for Elodie. How quickly he'd fallen completely for her. "I wish I could go with you."

"Me too." A small smile tipped her lips. "Perhaps when this is all done, we can enjoy long walks at your daughter's place. Watch Arik toss pebbles into the water?"

"I'd like that."

She smoothed out the wrinkles she'd made in the fabric of his shirt. "Do you want…more, you know, than Sierra?"

Her question shocked him. "Kids?"

She shrugged and nodded at the same time, and her cheeks flushed. "Yeah, I mean, I guess."

"It'd depend on if the person I'm with wants them."

"And if she does?" she asked quietly.

"Then I'd be ecstatic about trying." Pregnancy wasn't common in such long-lived beings. They could wait for two hundred years before a child was born, but he'd make sure to show his mate as much love in between as he would after.

She stepped back. "I'll be careful."

"I'll be waiting." She was about to pull away, but he grabbed her hand. "If something happens, I'll find you."

"I know. That's the only reason I'm okay being the bait."

She pulled him in for one last kiss before walking out the door.

He should sit his ass on the floor, but her evening walks made him nervous. He crept to the window and hunkered down. No lights were on in the house, and he couldn't see much better outside.

Elodie did a lazy stretch like she didn't have a care in the world. She shoved her hands into her pockets and walked down the drive.

Just as he was relaxing because he could still see her, a male swooped out of the sky, his wings spread wide. Ransom ripped the curtain down just as another person darted from the bushes separating her house from her neighbor's.

He tore out of the house as Elodie's scream ripped through the night. She was on the ground, kicking at the male who had swan-dived on her. The other male spotted Ransom.

"Get her out of here," he snarled to his partner. "I'll take care of him."

The first male bear-hugged Elodie so tightly she couldn't move, and they vanished.

"No!"

The second male, an enforcer who'd stepped down after Tosca had gotten a position as a senator, rounded on him.

The dull glint of silver flashed in what was left of the fading sunlight. Ransom charged. The male hesitated, then lowered into a crouch. He tried to slash out, but Ransom grabbed his arm, twisted it, and snapped the dagger from his hand.

The male was stunned. He cried out and cradled his arm, stumbling back. Ransom kicked his feet out from under him. When the guy toppled back, releasing another yell when a wing warped under him, Ransom dove. He flipped him over and knelt on the male's wings.

"Fuck! Get off me!" The guy tried to struggle, but his enforcer training was no match for Ransom's experience.

"I'm not some random Numen you've fucked with." Ransom smacked the male's head against the pavement. "Who sent you?"

The male yelled unintelligibly and snorted.

Ransom thumped his head again. "Who do you work for?"

"Fuck you."

Another smack. "Who?"

"Fuck—"

The next blow knocked the guy unconscious.

He'd heal quickly enough. Ransom pulled out his phone. Keeping the knife in one hand, he dialed with the other.

Urban picked up. "Yeah?"

"I've got one of them. One got away with Elodie."

"Where are you?"

"Her place."

The line went dead. The attacker groaned. Ransom curled his fingers through the male's hair. "Tell me everything you know."

"No."

Ransom made a shallow slice across his neck with the male's dagger. "I'm not afraid to test your healing power."

"Go for it." He tried to wiggle out from under him, but Ransom rammed his ass down on the busted wing. "I'm dead anyway."

Another yell rent the air.

Urban landed next to him, his gaze on the enforcer. "Torke, you fucker. What the hell'd you do now?"

"Fuck off, Urban."

Ransom cracked the male's head against the pavement again. "That's his favorite answer," he said to Urban.

Nothing but groaning filled the night.

Urban toed Torke's leg. "Come on, man. You've been busted. You really want to go down for some asshole senator?"

"You don't know him." Torke's voice shook.

Ransom exchanged a look with Urban. Their suspicions were confirmed.

Urban squatted at the male's head. "You'd be surprised what we've dealt with when it comes to senators."

"But you can walk away. The people he threatens can't."

Ransom eased his grip, but not enough so the male could move. "Your loved ones?"

"I have daughters."

"And you're okay with Elodie being abused in their place?" Ransom asked.

"She should've stayed out of it. My girls don't have a choice."

Urban shook his head. "What if we can help them and stop the person behind this?"

"You can't, warrior." Torke spat. "It goes too far up. No one will believe you."

"Up high, like Senator Thomas?" Ransom held his breath, waiting for an answer.

Torke's head was at an odd angle, but he blinked at Urban. "How do you…"

"His grandson was killed because he learned the truth," Urban said. "It wasn't hard to figure out, and it's why Elodie agreed to be bait. Tommy told her everything."

"She's dead already, then."

Rage burned through Ransom's veins. "Then help us save her, and we'll rescue your family."

"You can't. You have no way. He's connected in ways you can't imagine."

Urban ducked his head to meet Torke's eyes. "Can he do better than having a buddy who's in charge of the Daemon mines? Senator Thomas used to make deals with his sire."

Torke blinked again. "That's not possible."

Ransom's humorless laugh echoed through the night. "You'd be surprised what's possible. Senator Thomas has gotten away with it for too long."

"No." Torke shook his head, heedless of his nose brushing the ground. "No. I'm not the one who got to you. You might as well kill me, and maybe my daughters can be safe."

"Where are they now?" Urban asked.

"My mate took them to the human realm, but that male has his own watchers everywhere. One of the other enforcers' daughters was taken almost a year ago because of Senator Colbert's fuckup."

Ransom and Urban exchanged another glance. A

missing female, just as Sandeen suspected. Her disappearance could've been hidden by someone as powerful as the head senator.

"We have people everywhere too." Ransom said it with so much conviction it rang true. Sierra could make it happen with her technological capabilities.

"He'll find a way. Kill me."

"How many work under him?" Urban asked.

Torke went still, his gaze locked on to Urban's. "They're everywhere," he whispered.

Shadows scurried around them. Ransom glanced at Urban. The male's face was stone. "You called for reinforcements?" he asked quietly.

"They're on their way," he answered just as low.

So those movements weren't from their team.

Shit.

With a heave Ransom didn't think was possible, Torke pushed up. Ransom tumbled backward, and Torke lifted into the air. He dipped and soared, but Ransom had to let him go. He and Urban automatically put their backs together and withdrew a weapon for each hand.

Torke's knife felt unwieldy and unbalanced, but it was better than nothing.

"I see three," Ransom said under his breath.

"Four." As soon as the word left Urban's mouth, a shout came from overhead. A dark figure snatched Torke out of the sky. The male wailed, giving up the fight like it was the last thing he could do to save his family.

"Back to three," Urban said, resigned. They could've helped Torke, but they'd do their best to get to the male's family before their attackers did.

The figures lunged.

Ransom slashed and cut. The light was almost gone, so it was like fighting shadow beasts—clumsy and unaccustomed to hand-to-hand combat. Blood made the ground slick, but none of it was his. He doubted much, if any, was Urban's.

One attacker, a female, fell to her knees. Behind her, another surged forward. A fourth? Or would that be fifth?

"It's Bronx," the male said as he drew closer.

Another figure yanked at the attacker trying to slash between him and Urban. "And me," Jagger said. Ransom hadn't fought with the male until now.

The altercation was over almost before it started. Three attackers were on the ground. They'd all likely heal, and they'd all probably react like Torke—with panic and despair.

"I need to get to Elodie," Ransom said.

"We're tracking her," Bronx said grimly, and Ransom knew he meant Sierra but couldn't say her name. "But the bastard's transcending all over Earth like he knows we've got tabs on him."

Elodie must be terrified, but the constant movement probably meant she was still alive.

"They'll take her to the underworld." Ransom stepped away from the group. He had to find her. He'd given her his word.

"Sandeen's on it," Jagger said. "As soon as Tosca gets here, she'll get enforcers she trusts to deal with this crew and secure the realm."

Another figure swooped down from the sky. The director landed and scanned the dimly visible destruction. "Bloody hell."

After Urban filled him in, the director gave a firm nod. "I'll deal with the senator myself. Gladly. Get the whole team assembled on Earth and save Elodie. Let's finish this."

Ransom didn't need to be told twice. He transcended to his daughter's. His wrist wasn't burning with a sync mark.

He had to trust it meant Elodie was still okay. She was his, and if anyone were to be her mate, it would be him.

URBAN CHARGED toward the shop building on Sierra's property. Ransom was just ahead of him. Dionna was at the door, waiting for them. Jagger would arrive after he went with Director Vale to deal with Senator Thomas. Bronx was right behind.

Outside, Boone stood next to Dionna, with Arik on his hip. The boy was calm, used to seeing everyone coming and going.

Boone stepped aside. "She's in the computer room." His gaze drifted over Ransom. "Try not to get blood on the walls."

"Will do." Ransom sped inside. He was worried for Elodie; they all were. The blood spatter wasn't terrible. More on his hands than the rest of his clothing. And he'd clean the walls—after his female was safe.

The small building was filled with computers. Once the team realized they could have Sierra's talents back, they pooled their resources to build a separate place as far from the couple's cabin as possible, with as much security as they could offer. She wasn't just Ransom's daughter. Her family was their family.

Sandeen was leaning over the desk next to Sierra. Four bright screens blinked in their faces.

"Trinidad." Sierra's head swirled. "Shit. They disappeared."

Sandeen squinted. "They're disappearing for longer periods of time."

Ransom shouldered in. "The tracker was supposed to trace her into the Gloom."

"Sandeen tested it." Sierra clicked around. "But the Gloom has its own rules, and Sandeen has a different lineage than Elodie." A dot flashed on one of the lower screens. "There. Toronto."

"Are they afraid they're being followed?" Sandeen asked.

"Who could follow them like that?" Sierra shook her head. "Never mind. Senator Thomas would know what we're capable of."

"And it's gone." Sandeen pushed back from the desk. "They're going in and out of the Gloom. But he's an enforcer." He snapped his fingers. "He's passing her off to different demons. They were likely placed in areas with low warrior presence, waiting for the cue."

Sandeen frowned. "Demons aren't that organized."

Harlowe touched her mate's arm. "They are if a senator's controlling them."

Rage reddened Ransom's face. "And if he's got Numen working with demons because he's threatened their family."

"Unconscionable," Dionna said.

"If the tracker drops in the Gloom, then what?" Ransom asked.

Sandeen shook his head. "We have to search for her."

"How?" Urban asked. "The in-between realms don't really have locations, just, like, vibes."

The room went silent. The screen flashed again, and Ransom sagged. Urban would be tearing the Gloom apart if Persephone had been taken. He didn't know how Ransom was as rational as he was. It'd been clear they were into each other the few times Urban had seen them together. All the team members were worried. The longer she was gone, the more likely she'd experience something terrible.

"Cape Town," Sierra said. The dot blinked for several moments, then disappeared.

How many humans were seeing Elodie appear and disappear as some demon possessing a host yanked her into the Gloom with them?

"Who's closest to her?" Sandeen asked. "Who knows her best?"

Ransom absently rubbed his wrist. "I am."

"Then you come with me." Sandeen looked around the room. "You all come with me."

"All of us?" Dionna asked.

Sandeen wiggled his finger at the screen. "This is structured. I don't trust it."

"A trap?" Urban asked. Just what they fucking needed. An organized demon attack. "You think you can get us all into the Gloom?"

"Guess we'll find out."

Sierra looked to Dionna. "You go in there, I won't know what's going on."

"It's a risk we'll have to take," Dionna answered.

They piled outside. Harlowe snaked a hand over Urban's shoulder. "Hook arms. We'll be a regular warrior train."

Jagger jogged down the path toward them. "Hey, wait up."

The whole team was together, except for Sierra. Jagger fell in line behind Urban. He was dressed in tactical garb like the rest of them.

Urban held out an elbow. "What happened with the senator?"

Jagger clasped his hand around it, his expression grim. "Director Vale told him he was detaining him for treason. The senator pretended to be confused, then pulled a vial of angel fire on him." His smile was dark. "The director and I were ready for it. Unfortunately, the senator won't be answering for his crimes. He used the vial on himself."

The team fell quiet.

"Shit," Urban said. "But once we rescue Elodie, it's fucking done."

Anyone willingly working for the senator would be too afraid to do anything but live a normal Numen life. Anyone the senator had threatened would be safe.

"We've got to find her first," Ransom said.

"I get the hint," Sandeen said. "Think dark thoughts, and it'll help you cross."

Urban directed his anger toward Senator Thomas. The old senator was dead, but he deserved so much worse. He should've been bound and quartered—

A sour smell enveloped him, and a thousand tiny jabs hit his skin. He blinked and looked down.

Jagger wrinkled his nose. "Guess thinking about how I'd like to watch the senator die again did the trick."

"Same," Urban growled. He had the strongest urge to take a step forward, like someone was pushing him back out.

"You're going to have to stay connected," Sandeen said. "The realm will keep trying to expel you."

Yet the demons had figured out a way to keep the females in the realm. The senator's suggestions based on how the Mist worked?

"Let's find her." Ransom practically hauled them all forward.

Sandeen and Ransom led the way through fine yellowish droplets that stung their skin and left a spoiled-milk scent in the air. The Gloom was the Mist's opposite but had a similar heaviness. It left a person with the same lack of desire to stay. Nothing but mist and grass, though the grass in this realm was crusty and in a perpetual state of dying.

Dark shapes appeared ahead. Hair stood up on the back of Urban's neck.

"Fuck me," Jagger breathed. "They're surrounding us."

"Now's your chance to back out," Sandeen said.

"No fucking way," Ransom growled.

Urban and the others murmured their agreement.

"Yup, wanted to make sure." Sandeen scanned around them. "I want everyone committed to dying if I'm going in with you."

The demons were ready for them. They'd gathered in the Gloom, something that should've been impossible, but Urban was looking at it.

"Ransom!" Elodie screamed from behind the wall of demons. Another yelp left her, and a baby started crying.

"Ah," Sandeen said. "They wanted a female to take care of the baby."

The mother had died or been killed, and the demons probably didn't know which one of them had sired the child. The poor female. Even more reason to get out of this successfully. They'd give the girl's family peace and give the baby with the atrocious start to life a real chance at happiness.

"They're trying to surround us, so here's what we do," Dionna said quietly. "We rush the group hiding Elodie. We get her and the baby in the middle and make a three-sixty wall."

No one answered, but they tensed as a unit, withdrawing their knives.

Dionna lowered her chin, her gaze high like she was beginning a race. "Go!"

They ran at the first wall of demons. Urban and Jagger paired off since they were next to each other. Dionna and

Bronx did the same. Harlowe kept pace with Ransom as he barreled into the demons and tossed them to the side instead of battling one at a time.

Within minutes, they'd surrounded a crouching Elodie. She curled over the bundle in her arms, and Ransom stood over her. The rest of them formed a ring around her and took on the demons.

More dark figures came out of the mist. Urban thrust and stabbed, concentrating on maiming and keeping hold of his increasingly slippery daggers.

How many fucking creatures were there?

They'd been ready for a unit of seven. The senator had probably prepped them.

Grunts and snarls filled the air. The baby was no longer crying. Fuck, was that a bad thing? They couldn't come this far and lose either one.

Urban yanked his knife from the demon in front of him, but a wiry symaster slipped between them and slashed his abdomen.

Urban grunted against the agony searing through his body. He kicked at the symaster, but the archmaster he'd been grappling with stabbed his shoulder with a talon-tipped wing.

The seriousness of their situation sank in. They'd never fought this many underworld creatures at once. They weren't prepared, and they were cornered, keeping an angel and a baby safe.

Another claw raked his side.

He wasn't ready to die. He had so much he wanted to say to Persephone. So much time he wanted to spend with her. He'd wasted the last month, and now he might've lost whatever time he'd had left.

~

PERSEPHONE BOBBED one leg over the other. Today was her training team's last day in the field. She was in a bustling casino, not one of the ones she and Urban had hunted in. Memories of those days tugged at her heart, but the feelings weren't as heavy as they used to be. She missed him, and she looked forward to fully reconciling with him during her break.

Kadee skidded around a corner. "Percy."

The same name Urban sometimes called her. It was still special when he said it, but her team used it in the field. Her given name would stand out too much. The nickname blended better, and only a few people gave them more than a glance.

To anyone else, she looked like a local instead of a tourist. She wore shredded jeans and a shirt from a band that had done a residency in the casino. Her favorite boots fit the look too.

Persephone scooted over on her bench. She'd been pretending to be a local on a phone break, but she'd been watching a family milling in a souvenir store. Sylphs piled at their feet. One display had already been tipped, and she'd spotted the adolescent boy pocketing a key chain.

She'd been about to call it in when Kadee appeared.

"Have you heard?" Kadee hissed in her ear.

Frowning, Persephone shook her head. "No. What?"

"I heard Stana on the phone. She's calling all of us in for an update."

"Can we take care of that family first?" She discreetly nodded toward the store. The baby was wailing, the mom hollered at the boy, and security personnel hustled down the corridor. Shit. It was too late to get to them. Stana might have the team follow them home instead.

"No, listen. The realm is in turmoil."

The family pushed to the back of her mind, Persephone gawked at Kadee. "How?"

Mac and Molly trotted toward them. "We have to get back," he said.

Kadee motioned for the pair to hurry closer. When Mac crouched in front of them and Molly leaned in, she whispered, "The senate is in an uproar, and Senator Thomas was killed."

Persephone's mouth dropped open. "What? How?"

They crowded so close their foreheads almost touched. Kadee continued, "I couldn't hear all of it, but Stana said 'traitor' like she didn't believe it. But get this, she says, 'You expect me to believe the oldest male in the senate was trafficking our females and working with demons?'"

Persephone leaned back, her eyes wide. Was this what Urban couldn't tell her? He'd been upset about their relationship, but he'd still helped to uncover the biggest conspiracy in the realm's history.

If she could be half the warrior he was, she'd be proud.

Mac shook his head. "No. That's impossible." He scoffed. "Come on."

Molly nodded. "I agree. Senator Thomas has served the realm—"

"You don't know the whole story." Persephone chewed her lower lip. What should she tell them? The information was confidential, but they were her teammates. They worked to save the realm too. "I don't even know the whole story, but I experienced some of it."

She decided to spill. To tell them everything about Senator Colbert. They almost didn't believe her about Sandeen, but he'd been glimpsed a few times in the realm. Rumors had spread.

Kadee's eyes were saucers. "I had no idea."

Persephone shrugged. "I know. I don't really agree with

the secrecy. I've heard a lot from my parents over the years that I thought wasn't good to keep from the Numen public." But that was an issue for another time. "Where does Stana want us to me—"

Burning pain etched the skin of her wrist. She hissed, then brought her wrist into view.

Her eyes went wide. Kadee's expression flashed from confusion to astonishment. She grabbed Persephone's arm. "Is that a brand?"

The others inspected her wrist while Persephone numbly looked on. An urge to leave, to go somewhere, built inside her, but she didn't know where. "I've got to go."

Molly sucked in a breath. "Your assigned mate is in trouble."

Persephone looked from her friend to her brand. Assigned mate. She wanted nothing but to get to Urban, to find him and take care of whatever was wrong. And wasn't that how it worked?

Frustrated, she racked her brain. Everyone knew how the sync brand functioned, but no Numen really expected it to happen. Sudden brands weren't common. For the most part, Numen were allowed to choose their mates if they wanted to mate. But mates could heal, and if she got the half wing on her skin, then her mate was in trouble.

"It's Urban." She rose. There was no time for relief.

Kadee stood. "Where?"

"I don't know." She palpated her mark, willing it to give her more information. "I need to go outside and find a place to ascend."

Kadee nodded. "I'm coming with you."

She shook her head. "You have orders to follow. Please let Stana know what happened." She spun and raced for an exit.

Mac caught up with her. "We're going too." Kadee appeared on her other side.

She wanted to stop and talk sense into them, but the urgency grew. "You can't. You'll get in trouble."

Molly fell in step with them. "I think it's clear we don't care. We're a unit. The rest of our team will understand that we can't let you walk alone into what might be a dangerous situation."

Dangerous. She hadn't considered that. "I don't want you all getting into harm's way. You're almost done."

"Nope." Kadee clasped her hand, and they pushed through the exit. "There's an open stairwell in the parking garage. It has a blind spot on the second floor, and we won't have to worry about cameras."

"We're staying hooked together," Molly said. "Where you go, we go."

"I don't know where I'm going." They couldn't transcend to an unknown place. Did the mark override that? It would be the only way one could reach their mate to aid in their healing.

"Exactly," Kadee said.

They stopped on the second-floor landing. No other footsteps sounded. The team crowded into a corner, and Persephone concentrated on the urgency inside her.

"Take me to him," she said as she took a step, keeping a fierce grip on her teammates' hands.

A sour smell enclosed her. Prickles stung her skin, and she blinked her eyes open. The air burned her skin and eyes.

Kadee coughed next to her. "What is this place?"

The grass beneath their feet was dead, and the stench of rot surrounded them. The opposite of the Mist.

"It's the Gloom." Awe and fear tainted Mac's voice.

Snarls sounded. Yells from familiar voices. She spotted a gaggle of warriors surrounded by dark forms.

They weren't dressed in their warrior uniforms, but they'd come ready to fight. Persephone pulled daggers from holsters under her jeans and rushed forward. "This way."

A grisly sight became visible. So many demons. She made out the warriors from Urban's team. They fought in a circle, protecting something at their backs. Covered in blood and gore, they slashed and cut. Destroyed demons lay scattered at their feet. The warriors had probably used all their angel fire, but more demons surrounded them.

How were any of them still standing?

Her gaze landed on Urban. His face was slack, but he still fought. The black material he wore had a wet gleam. His blood? Much of it had to be. He was pale, and he wasn't using one of his arms.

She wanted to shout for him, but her training kicked in. *Analyze the situation.* None of the warriors could leave the Gloom. They were pinned in place and couldn't transcend out of it. Same with whatever—whoever—they were protecting.

The archmasters were just as wounded, but they outnumbered the angels, and fighting had drained the warriors' resources.

"We go in at one point like a wedge," Persephone spoke only loud enough for her team to hear. "Make a hole so whatever they're protecting can get out and they can evacuate the most injured."

Kadee brandished two of her knives. "You take care of Urban; we'll have your back."

Persephone readied herself for an armed sprint. "Now!"

They raced into the fray. Urban fell to his knees just as he caught sight of them. He blinked like he couldn't believe his eyes, but Persephone couldn't waste time. A demon towered over him, pulling his talons back like he was going to try to swipe off Urban's head in one pass.

Persephone tucked the handle of one of her knives in her mouth, yanked off the vial around her neck, and charged. She dumped the contents on the demon's head and kicked him in the chest. Roaring, he stumbled back. Another demon advanced, its head down to impale her with its horns.

Mac jumped between her and it. "Save your mate."

Her mate.

She dropped in front of him, trusting her team to protect them. His head was hanging. A large gash bisected his abdomen, and she didn't like what she saw. Her stomach threatened to revolt.

"Urban. Urban?" She lifted his head; his eyes were blurry. "I'm here. What do I do?"

She wasn't trained for this. To have a mate and be the only one who could save him. She wouldn't quit trying, but did she save him here? Could she drag him out?

Dionna pushed toward them, hacking off a demon's hand on the way. "Your wings."

Persephone's wings were still morphed. She had a human shirt on. Her terror must've shown. Dionna hauled her and Urban up. "Think about a safe place in Numen and go there."

The only place she could think of was home. Just as Dionna shoved them to take a step, the pressure around them lightened. The arrival of new fighters had helped the warriors' morale and their energy surged.

She anchored her arms around Urban and dragged him a step, concentrating on her home. How the green grass was plush and healthy and not sick and withered. Another step and the stinging droplets turned into sunshine. The clash of yells and snarls became the chirps of birds. Her parents' house loomed over them.

She stumbled, and Urban went with her, upsetting her balance. "Stay up, big guy," she groaned, but his weight sank like a stone in the bathtub.

What should she do? They were always told mates could help heal each other faster, but how? Something about the wings. "Help! Mother! Father!"

"Persephone?" Mother's face appeared in the window, then she was gone. Only seconds later, she was running out the back door.

Relief poured through Persephone. "How do I heal him?"

Her wings. She tore at her shirt, but that meant letting Urban go. A long moan left him, and he tried to catch himself, but he'd used the immobile arm with muscle and tendon showing.

Seams ripped but not fast enough. She whipped the shirt over her head and tossed it aside. The human bra was a pain, but seconds later, she had enough room to unfurl her wings from their morph.

Mother raced to their side and dropped to her knees, her eyes wide and her face ashen. "Y-you, uh…" Mother squeezed her eyes shut. "Drape them over him and think about your healing power and how he needs it and how you want him to have it."

Persephone leaned over her mate, her hands on his back, and thought about all his wounds and how she'd mend them. Without her healing, he'd have lingered, his body trying and failing, again and again, to repair some of the damage with what little energy he had left before he succumbed altogether.

"That's it," Mother said quietly next to her. "Keep going."

Comforting heat bloomed around them, and Persephone kept imagining how Urban should be healing. Another moan left him, but less pained this time. A groan.

"U-Urban?" She wished she could keep the shaking out of her voice. "Hey, baby. Come back to me, okay?"

His breathing was less ragged, but he was curled on his side on the ground where he'd collapsed. Other than the noises coming from him, he hadn't moved.

"I've been matched with you, but you don't have to mate me. You can just, you know, keep doing your thing and I'll keep doing mine. All I ask is that you listen to my jokes."

He twitched. She barely heard him say her name.

"Yeah?" Her whole body trembled. Energy radiated from her. She'd give every last shred to help him.

His words came out raspy. "What do you call a well-balanced horse?"

Shocked, she said, "What?"

"Stable." A sigh left him.

Mother's shadow fell over them. "Did he just tell a joke?"

"Yes," Urban said with a groan. "And when I can get up again, I'm not letting your daughter go. You'll just have to live with it."

"What are you saying, Urban?" The healing energy had started to fade. If he was good enough to tell a joke, he could heal on his own. She'd need to recuperate and check on her teammates and his. He'd want to do the same. "Never mind. Now's not the time. Just rest, and Mother and I will get you somewhere more comfortable."

"I'm saying you're mine, Persephone. If you'll have me."

"Yes. You're mine, and I have the brand to prove it."

Mother patted them both. "Good, good. Now let's get you two into a bed to finish healing."

CHAPTER 18

Chaos surrounded Ransom. Just when he thought they'd come all this way only to fail, to lose the child and everyone else, a breath of not exactly fresh air had blown in. An ease in the press of demons around them.

"Get them out of here!" Jagger yelled in his ear and stepped in front of him to hack at a charging archmaster.

Sandeen jumped next to him, and the two warriors created an opening.

"Ransom?" Elodie's voice rose over the din. She cowered over the baby, using her body to take any blows directed their way. She peeked up at him, her terrified gaze wide.

"I'm here." He squatted next to her. "You have to stand. We need to get out of here now."

She nodded and stood on shaking legs, the baby bundled in its filthy rags held safely in her arms. Was the child okay? It couldn't possibly be asleep.

Harlowe glanced over her shoulder, where she was fighting next to Dionna. "Go."

It was one word, but he heard the rest she didn't say.

Don't worry about us. We'll know where to find you. Don't you dare come back and try to help.

The fight was waning. More warriors had arrived. Ransom didn't know how, but they were an answered prayer. Four, since he couldn't find Urban. Hopefully he'd been synced with a mate and she'd rescued him.

Hopefully, it'd been Persephone.

He hugged his arms around Elodie and the baby and pulled them out of the Gloom. Fresh Montana air surrounded them, and trees towered over their heads. In the distance, the scream of a red-tailed hawk resounded through the partly cloudy sky.

Elodie's breathing was ragged. He turned her to face him.

"Are you okay?"

She blinked up at him. "Is it over?" Blood smeared her cheeks, and her clothes were ripped. They'd barely gotten to her in time.

"Almost," he answered honestly. "Some warriors arrived to help. Saved our asses, basically."

He'd never heard of an organized attack by demons. "Organized" might be a strong word, but the creatures rarely worked together. Like Sandeen had said, someone was working with them, leading them, and it'd been Senator Thomas all along. It took him centuries to make demons do his bidding, but in the end, he'd failed. That was all that mattered.

The loss would dissuade demons from rising up. They could scurry back to their underworld caves and rot.

The drone of a four-wheeler sounded in the distance. Sierra's silhouette appeared with the machine, and as she neared, he could see her expression was set and determined. She killed the engine a few yards from them, probably not wanting to scare the baby.

Ransom lightly moved the rags from the baby's face. "Is it okay?"

"I think…" Elodie licked her lips and grimaced. She was covered in splatter. Turning, she spat, and the baby let out a contented sigh. "I think it's sleeping. I don't know if it's a boy or girl—the demons kept the child and wanted me to nurse it. They didn't understand I couldn't."

"What happened?" Sierra asked as she drew closer.

He didn't know if his daughter was up to date on everything. His focus had been Elodie when he'd been here last. "Elodie learned that Senator Thomas was behind it all. His grandson learned about a lot of it, and the senator killed him for it." The lack of regard from the elderly male still sent grim shivers down Ransom's spine. How could the male be responsible for so much death and violence?

Sierra nodded. "I pieced some of that together, but the director called to check on your status. He filled in the rest."

"When we found Elodie in the Gloom, there was an ambush."

Sierra frowned, worry across her face. "They worked together?"

"Yes." Enough to overwhelm warriors accustomed and armed to fight only one or two demons at a time.

"Shit." She approached Elodie. "And the baby?"

"Sleeping, I think." Elodie's concerned gaze searched Sierra's. "Do you think it's used to the noise and violence? How would that affect it?" She wrinkled her nose and pulled some of the filthy cloth farther away from the child. "Her."

"She looks to be a couple months old," Ransom said. "About when Sandeen found the discarded bloody robes."

Sierra grimaced as she pulled the rags back, then recoiled. "She needs a bath and clean clothes, poor thing.

Boone stocked some formula in case a baby was located." Her expression turned serious. "The director thinks he knows who her mother was. A female named Gabrielle. She was a couple hundred years old and a bit of a loner. No mate. No family."

"No family. We'll make one for her."

The little girl's blue eyes opened. She gurgled and stretched before falling back to sleep.

"Poor Gabrielle," Elodie said. "I knew of her. She was quiet. Content. She made blankets to sell in the market, but I hadn't seen her for a while. A convenient target for assholes like Senator Thomas." She traced a finger down the baby's cheek. "What were they feeding her?"

Sierra's lips curled in a grimace. "It might be better not to know."

Ransom peered at the perfect little halfling. Her mother had been a survivor to last long enough to give birth to the baby. He only hoped Gabrielle had heard talk of Sandeen and knew her baby could grow to be decent, even if she never left Daemon.

The last part was no longer a concern.

"Will life in Numen be a hard adjustment for her?" Elodie asked.

"Perhaps, but I'll be there for her." He gave her an encouraging smile. "I've done this before."

"You are the reigning expert," Sierra agreed. "I hate to change the subject, but how are the others?"

"I don't know." His moment of relief vanished. "It was dire, then the tide turned. Urban was badly injured before the rest of the team arrived, but he was gone when we left."

"Sync mate?" Sierra asked.

Ransom shrugged, wishing he had more answers. The hard part in any battle was that one person couldn't be all things to everyone. His role had been to assure Elodie's safety and rescue the baby with her. The rest… His chest grew heavy. "Perhaps. More warriors arrived. Did you tell another team about us?"

Sierra shook her head. "I'll get back to the house and find out everything." She'd work her surveillance magic and have answers within minutes. "Go to the house and take care of yourselves and the baby."

He sensed Elodie needed some time before she had to be around others. She'd been through a lot, and her senses and emotions were overwhelmed. He was with her, and the baby was content. "We'll take our time getting back."

His daughter fired up the engine and drove off.

"Thank you," Elodie murmured. "I need a minute."

"Let's sit for a while."

She sank to her bottom at the side of the path that ran to Sierra and Boone's place. Ransom sat next to her.

"We should give her a name." He ran his fingers over the dirty wraps, wishing he could strip off his shirt and swaddle her in it, but the cloth around her was cleaner than he was. "Whatever one they used can be left behind."

"I feel like we should honor her mother."

His sweet El. "How about Rielle? Named for Gabrielle, but not enough to give her identity away."

She gazed at him, her brow crinkling. "I want to be a part of her life." She opened her mouth and closed it again.

He didn't know what she was going to say, but he knew what was missing from what she had said. "I want you in her life. And…in mine."

A cautious smile chased away the shadows in her eyes. "Really?"

"I can't imagine going back to things as they were and not having you walk through the door."

"You're probably sick of my house." Her lips twisted.

"I'm sick of my house after waiting for weeks to get attacked in it."

"I've got a big place—and it's already raised one strong female. I think it's strong enough for two more." He tipped her chin up, leaned in, and kissed her. They were dirty and grimy and covered in demon blood, but he needed to touch her. "I've fallen in love with you, El," he said against her lips.

"Oh, Ransom. I've had a thing for you since you chased me into the Mist." She pressed one more kiss on his lips and hugged the baby closer. "Let's go find out how everyone's doing while Rielle's sleeping. Then we can clean her up."

The walk didn't take long, and when they reached the big cabin, Sierra met them at the door like she'd been planning to go find them.

"You've got word?" His heart hammered. He might have just experienced the best moment of his life, declaring his love to a female he wanted to spend eternity with, only to find out his team was suffering.

"Urban is healing with Persephone at her parents' place. The extra warriors were her fellow trainees. They ignored orders and followed her, and since they saved you, I don't think they'll be too badly reprimanded."

"They'd better not," he growled. His protective nature extended to those young angels who'd charged into battle with almost no information but that a fellow warrior might need help.

Sierra's smile was brief. The whole team likely felt the same way. "Sandeen said all the demons are down, and when he stormed the underworld, he killed more to drive home the point: Senator Thomas is no longer around to feed them females and angel fire. The rest of the warriors have been healed by their mates." She shrugged. "Good thing they've all been synced by now. The director has been briefed, and there'll be a meeting when everyone's recovered."

"So it's over?" Elodie asked, hope in her voice.

"So damn much is over," Sierra said, triumphant. Her smile fell. "I guess the rest is up to you and the director—what you want to tell and how much."

Elodie gazed down at Rielle. Her tiny mouth had fallen open, and she was sleeping hard. "I think we'll have to be very careful with what to share. There are innocents who need to be kept safe. Who'll always be targets if we're not cautious."

"I agree." Sierra exchanged a relieved look with Ransom. "Would you two like to rest here for a few days until a story is laid out for how you two ended up together with a baby?"

"I'd like that." More than anything, he wanted to spend time with his family. He needed to know that this would be the beginning of a long life with the ones he loved.

THE WARM BODY Urban woke up to had him hard and aching. He wrapped an arm around her waist and hugged her closer. She murmured, waking from the deep slumber they'd shared.

He took a few steady breaths, and realization set in. Where he was. Who he was with. And more importantly, why. The details crystalized, and he freed his arms from the blankets and the warm skin of the female who had helped hold him up in the shower before they crawled into bed. The shades were drawn over the French doors, but there was enough ambient light to highlight the mating mark on his wrist.

Persephone rolled over and watched him cautiously. "I knew it was you as soon as I saw it. I could feel that you were in trouble."

"I was in a lot of trouble." He tucked himself back under the covers, facing her, and pulled the blankets up to their shoulders. "And now you're mine."

She searched his face. "We don't have to mate."

"Are you kidding? I thought I was fucked, and not spending every minute I could with you was my biggest regret."

"Urban," she whispered. "Really?"

"Never doubt it. I'll never give you a reason to again." He brushed his hand up her side, hoping the door was locked. They hadn't dressed after the shower, so he assumed they had some level of privacy. "Thank you for saving me."

"Thank you for not dying."

He tugged her close. Her bare breasts pushed into his other arm, which he wedged under her until he was holding her. "About what I said earlier…"

Her fingertips trailed over his face and down his neck. "What, exactly?"

"About not wanting to do anything with you while your parents are under the same roof. How about we table that for now but be really quiet?"

She pushed him onto his back. "I'm the one who proved she could be quiet. It's your turn."

Crawling over him, she spread her wings behind her. A glorious sight. High, full tits that he palmed immediately. For weeks, he'd worried he'd never get to do this again. He'd never get to trace her scars—with his tongue—or feel her explode against him.

She rocked herself over him. No need to prepare; she

was growing wetter with each stroke. "Urban." She tipped her head back, her tangled, tousled hair falling behind her.

He gripped her hips and guided her onto his erection. When she sank down, he couldn't take his eyes from where he was disappearing inside her. "This. I want this as often as possible. I want us to be bonded." He thrust his hips up, and she moaned. "Quiet, remember?"

She gave him a playful scowl, rose until he was almost out of her, then swirled her hips. He bit back a groan. "This was a bad idea—no, it's the best idea."

"So good," she breathed.

Only low grunts and groans left them, a little whimper from her when she got close. He slid his hand between them and stroked her clit as she rode. Her explosion was imminent when she leaned over, draping her wings over their bodies like a privacy curtain.

Their lips met in a needy flurry, capturing each other's sounds. His release hit fast and hard, and she came at the same time. It was perfect. His promise to her. He'd never leave her again. Never let her down. Never disappoint her. Just like she had done for him.

"I love you, Persephone," he murmured against her lips.

She opened her eyes, those beautiful brown irises full of his future. "I love you too, Urban."

They lay together for several minutes, basking in the afterglow.

"So, now what?" she asked.

"What do you mean?" He was ready to fuck her again, but the fatigue of recovery still hung heavy on him, and he was content to hold her.

"I disobeyed orders. Stana called us in."

"You got the brand. That trumps everything."

She relaxed only slightly. "Kadee, Mac, and Molly came

with me. I couldn't talk them out of it. They didn't even tell Stana until afterward. I won't let them face punishment."

That might be a little trickier. "They saved us, Persephone. You didn't just save me, but you and your fellow trainees saved my team. We were ambushed and outnumbered."

"Demons shouldn't be able to do that."

"Senator Thomas enabled them. The director will go to bat for your team. Stana's probably only worried about setting an example, but this time they set a good example. You four functioned as a small, competent warrior team."

She lifted her head, and a wing fluttered behind her. He almost asked if she hurt, but he kept his mouth shut. She'd repeatedly shown him she could take care of herself. "We did, didn't we? I didn't even have time to be scared."

"I'll tell you about everything while we lie in bed and recover. And have a lot of sex."

"Mm." She draped herself over him again, her wings forming a blanket. "I like the sound of that."

"We just need to know how everyone else is doing."

A knock thudded on the door. Persephone popped her head up. "Yes?"

"Just to let you know, the director stopped by. Everyone made it out and is healing. We'll meet in the evening to figure out what to do. So…take your time getting ready or…whatever."

"Thanks, Mother." Persephone rested her head on his chest and giggled. "Well, that part's taken care of. And they know."

"They totally know. In that case." He flung the covers away and crawled over her. "Let's do it again."

The sync ceremony was more for show than anything else. Urban was as committed to his mate as ever, and no official words could change it. They wore each other's sync brand, and he'd never known it was possible to be this deeply in love. Months had gone by while news about the senator and a carefully edited but nearly complete story spread through the realm.

The chatter had been loud, but when daily life hadn't changed, it died down. Urban didn't want drama overshadowing their mating celebration, so he and Persephone had waited, making his empty house into a cozy home in the interim.

Persephone glowed like the angel she was. She wore a backless gown to expose her scars, unashamed. The glint of her vial of angel fire was more like jewelry than a weapon. She was a warrior even in mating, and he wouldn't have it any other way.

He twined his hands with hers as Director Vale finished the ceremony.

When the words were concluded and Urban had kissed

Persephone in front of their friends and her family—his wasn't invited—his boss looked around. "This is how it all started."

"How do you mean?" Persephone asked. Then she snapped her fingers. "Oh, right. You and Odessa had your ceremony here when you were forced to take a mate. I remember that." She winced. "I came for the drama that night."

"It was dramatic," he agreed. "Enough to get a stubborn bugger like me to accept a mate. Best bloody decision I ever was forced to make. Isn't that right, Leo?"

Smiling indulgently, the former warrior director walked toward them, moving nimbly in his new prosthetic legs and not bothering to hide them with a floor-length robe. Millie, his mate, was tucked into his side.

"Senator," Urban said.

Leo shook his head. "It's going to take some time to get used to it. Never thought I'd wear that title. Never wanted to."

"Makes you perfect for it," Persephone said.

Millie nodded. "I said the same thing. I doubt Senator Thomas was ever like Leo, even when he was young centuries ago. Leo's experience makes him qualified to help lead this realm and protect everyone in it."

Director Vale's gaze drifted over Urban's shoulder. "And with our newest senate reporter, the senate will have a hard time keeping secrets."

Ransom gave a wave when he noticed the group staring at him. The little baby on Elodie's hip waved her chubby arm. Urban took in the sight. As much as Elodie had wanted to tell the realm everything, she knew there were some truths that wouldn't aid the realm but would only hurt those involved. Their new daughter was one. Sierra and her family were the other. Any fallen who'd survived their fall and moved on were given peace if they asked for it. Others were reunited with family who'd been forbidden from acknowledging their existence. A lot of healing needed to take place.

Elodie would be training more senate reporters to keep from becoming a target herself and to make the profession as objective as possible, as tamperproof as possible.

A hard hand clapped Urban's shoulder, and Bronx grinned at him. "Congrats, man. Hear we're going back in the field like the old days."

"The team is back together," Urban agreed.

Persephone grinned. "Urban's been talking nonstop. Are you all as excited as he is?"

"A schedule and more time at home?" Bronx shot Tosca an indulgent grin. "Hell yes. My enforcer said she can finagle her days off to match mine."

Jagger walked by, giving his congratulations. "See you in a couple weeks. The demons bugging Atlanta won't know what hit them." He glanced at Persephone. "What region are you working in?"

"Las Vegas." Persephone was still on her probation team. Director Vale had offered her a chance to work with Urban's team after she was done, but she'd passed. She would go on a team with Kadee, Mac, and Molly.

Urban had seen how well she and her friends functioned together. They needed to be together. It was best for them and for the realm.

Dionna and her mate swung in for congratulations. "I'm really happy for you. I'm thrilled to have our team back and that you have the support of strong mates."

Persephone beamed. Dionna didn't give out empty compliments.

Sandeen elbowed into the group. "I'm included in that, I hope."

Dionna narrowed her eyes at him, but her lips twitched. He was like a bonus member of the team, switching with Ransom when he needed to be around for his daughter.

The group moved on when the buffet opened.

When they were alone for a few moments, Urban pulled Persephone into his arms. "You're so damn beautiful, Percy."

"And you're so damn handsome, mate."

He'd never tire of hearing that. "You're all mine."

She tipped her face up. "Likewise."

Her mother appeared at her shoulder. "I'm really proud of you two. The changes in the realm are encouraging. We've never had a brighter future." Her eyes glittered. "And it's because of my daughter. I never would've imagined it, but I should've. I should've seen your potential from the beginning."

"Mother." Persephone embraced her, then gave her father a big hug. They were all wiping tears.

Urban inclined his head. Without Persephone's parents, they wouldn't have made the progress they had.

Her father put an arm around his mate. "We wanted to check if our weekly meal was still on with the busy week."

Persephone nodded. "It's at our place."

The meal was a standing event, but that wasn't the only time Urban and Persephone hung out with her parents. Their place was like a second home.

Her mother clapped her hands. "I'm going to get in line for food. Elodie's parents supplied the best mangos." She squeezed their linked hands. "Welcome to the family, Urban."

His parents might've half-ass abandoned him, but his team was his family and this female only expanded it. The difference was that she was the hub he orbited around.

"Knock, knock," he said.

Persephone grinned. "Who's there?"

"Olive."

"Olive who?"

"Olive you, and I don't care who knows it."

———

DEAR READER,

Thank you for joining me on the Angel Fire journey. We made it to the end! If you want more paranormal romance from me, you can start with some wolf shifters in Fever Claim. You can grab the book when you sign up for my newsletter where you'll also have access to my bonus material, sneak peeks, and photos of my pets.

THANK you so much for reading. I'd love to know what you thought. Please consider leaving a review of Eternal Fire.

ABOUT THE AUTHOR

Marie Johnston lives in the upper-Midwest with her husband, four kids, and an old cat. Deciding to trade in her lab coat for a laptop, she's writing down all the tales she's been making up in her head for years. An avid reader of paranormal romance, these are the stories hanging out and waiting to be told between the demands of work, home, and the endless chauffeuring that comes with children.